TEMPTING THE BILLIONAIRE
Twisted Billionaires #4

Blair Babylon

He's trying to start a Mafia war. *Who does that?*

Micah Shine is tall, handsome as hell, exudes wealth, and has just enough mischief in his shimmering eyes that I'm not sure I'll ever be able to really trust him.

He conned me. He trapped me. And now I'm on the run from the Mafia with him. I should have been more careful. But he's more than just a partner in crime to me now.

I'm falling in love, the head-over-heels type of love that's willing to overlook red flags. The kind that refuses to acknowledge how much power he has. How much access to documents and information that he shouldn't be able to get. The kind that knows that Micah Shine is no ordinary con man.

He's sweet to me. He's kind. And he's freaking magic in bed. But game recognizes game, and I can't help but wait for him to change the rules all over again.

The epic conclusion to the
Conning the Billionaire/Tempting the Billionaire Duet!

PRAISE FOR BLAIR BABYLON

PRAISE FOR CONNING THE BILLIONAIRE, MICAH #1

"Micah and Kylie are fire from the beginning!! The attraction is mutual, and the things they get up to had me fanning myself!!! So many pieces to the big con that Micah and Kylie are playing, of course ends up with mob bosses and mafia families, (its Atlantic City after all!!) Add lots of subterfuge and plans that don't go exactly as planned, and this story becomes a very funny, action packed, train wreck of amazing - ness !!! Can you read it as a stand alone?? Probably. But then you wouldn't know all the players, or all of the little," Easter eggs", that are dropped here and there from previous books. And those are AMAZING!!!!" ~ Amazon Reviewer

"WOW! This is a "seat of your pants" wild ride. Throughout this story, I put the book aside several times, shaking my head, wondering "what the ..." Con is the name of the game and both Kylie and Micah have mastery, but Micah excels at the game." ~ Amazon Reviewer

REVIEWS OF ROGUE, MAXENCE BOOK #1

"**Maxence is everything I love in a romance novel** - a whipsmart man with an anguishing call to serve that conflicts with his love for Dree. I was spellbound!" - New York Times bestselling author Julia Kent

"What a wild and sexy race through Paris! Rogue masterfully combines nail biting suspense with high steam for the ride of your life with Maxence and Dree." ~ USA Today bestselling author JJ Knight

"Another masterpiece from Blair Babylon, who I am convinced keeps getting better and better. Max is not at all as I'd imagined him, and really it's no wonder, since he has been forced to repress who he is. The real Max keeps popping up his head, doing real-Max things that the other Max wishes he wouldn't do. He struggles with his inner demons to be a Godly man, but he hasn't quite figured out how to balance the different parts of himself, and as a result, tortures himself. He is a man searching for himself, impeded by too many bad guys who wish him harm. It's hard to focus on self-actualization while trying to simply survive without getting yourself killed." -- E.C., Goodreads Reviewer

"Blair's stories have always been hot but this one might be the hottest yet." -- Xtreme Delusions Book Blog

"I just couldn't stop reading! This book is addictive!" -- Kat, Goodreads Reviewer

"Rogue is a phenomenal romantic suspense that is sure to delight and entertain as it holds your heart and mind captive. Nothing can prepare you for the roller coaster ride that is Maxence. He will take you unawares and leave you completely breathless and wanting. If nothing else, you will learn why he is so addicting to the women that he meets." -- Words Are The Breath of Life Book Blog

"Good gosh! Author Blair Babylon is a master at building suspense. I have been eagerly awaiting Maxence's story for YEARS. Finally it arrives and I am practically salivating as I tear into the book, excited that I will finally learn the truth about the elusive Maxence. As I am reading, I am finding that Maxence's unveiling is happening at the rate of an excruciatingly slow strips tease. The end of "Rogue" finds me with almost as many questions regarding who Maxence is as the beginning of the book-- but I promise that slooowly he is starting to be unveiled. **One thing that is made abundantly clear is that Maxence lives two polar opposite lives and this results in my finding myself even MORE intrigued by him. Now THIS is what I consider phenomenal writing!**" -- Lil Miss Reads A Lot Book Blog

ONE NIGHT IN MONACO

"Holy Maxence! Max hotness! Max suspense! Max everything! Follow your favorite book boyfriends Casimir and Arthur as they try to figure out WHAT the hell happened to Maxence in Monaco, with all the opulence and lavish lifestyle you'd expect from Blair Babylon's Runaway Billionaires. This series starter is hot, hot, hot!"
  ~~ USA Today bestselling romance author JJKnight

"Blair!! LOVED it! A fun, sexy, fast-paced read that had me on the edge of my seat wanting to know what happened that night!"
  ~~ Pippa Grant, USA Today BestsellingAuthor

"What I love about Blair Babylon books is the worlds she creates, and One Night in Monaco is no exception. Luxury, power, wealth - all of it beyond your dreams - is a backdrop for our very human, very vulnerable, and often extremely alpha characters who show us how uniquely human we all are -- but Maxence? He's one of a kind. And hot. Whooooo boy."

-- New York Times bestselling author Julia Kent

"Addictively entertaining and full of escapist goodness,this stylish page-turner left me breathless and begging for more!"

~~New York Times bestselling author Annika Martin

"This is *One Night In Monaco,* Billionaires In Disguise; Maxence written by the amazing Blair Babylon! This book has been a long awaited one! I'm so excited to finally dig into the man of mystery Maxence Grimaldi!! He has been in this series as friends of Casimir and Arthur, his sexy as h@ll friends from boarding school. Ms Babylon knows how to string you along and NEED to know about her wonderful characters. She never fails to amaze me with the amount of details and little flashes of other friends that she sprinkled throughout her books. Full of intrigue, sinister associates, mob related activity, utter indulgence of opulence and sexy sexy times! Hurry up with the next one Ms Babylon! I'm about to burst over here!!"

--Goodreads Reviewer

"I knew that I would be drawn into another great series and it definitely got me out of the book funk I was in. Ms Babylon is an author who literally creates a world to escape into thats way out of my normal life, but so totally believable too. This book took me from the monotonous dreary reality of work, and whisked me to the cosmopolitan shores of Monaco and Italy. Max is a character that has been in a few of the other books in the Billionaire world, hes always been a bit of an enigma and I can't wait to read the next book in his series. I haven't read every book in this vast world of European Elite and Royal society, but if you want to get hooked then you can start with a book 1 in a few of the storylines free... What are you waiting for. Get hooked like me. What I thought to One night in Monaco... Well I read it in one sitting, every page was more intriguing than the first. MAX has been a favourite character for a while, he's so mysterious and I can't wait to read the next books."

-- Goodreads Reviewer

"Friends, Casimir, Arthur and Maxence, will do anything for the other. Max is missing...His friends fear the worst, when they look for Max, always coming up empty handed...Until Genoa Italy happened. Maxence, always the gentleman and rescuer, was needed by Simone. He would do anything to help get her home, where she will be safe. I want to thank, Blair Babylon, for bringing Max's story to life. I can't wait until the next episode. This most definitely gets 5 stars."

-- Goodreads Reviewer

BLAIR BABYLON'S BOOKS

"The book oozed heart and passion from every page, it was as if it was traveling through my fingers to touch my very soul - I'm gobsmacked at how I feel about it! It showed more than I thought I was going to get it gave me *love and passion in absolute bin loads and moreover it was full of desire, hope, longing, honesty and devotion* - not just from the characters but from the author also because her devotion to her craft was clearly evident in this book - she nailed it!!" --

"**The chemistry Wulf and Raegan have is amazing** and the fact that they are both so stubborn makes their relationship funny at times. The series covers everything from finding out about the good, bad, and ugly of each other to meeting the family. There are raw emotions in these books." ~~*Random Musesomy Book Blog*

"Blair Babylon knows what she is doing. **This is some of the best romance I have read, hands down.** It's got a little bit of everything, for everyone....the story was so well written, infused with sex, humor and drama, that **I would gladly read it over and over again.**" ~*Contagious Reads Blog*

"**If I could give 10 stars I would!** I adore this book, I have read it two times completely and many times parts of it." ~*Katrina's Books Blog*

"**AWESOME!** When I first started reading this book I thought it was going to be your regular romance book and I thought, what kind of spin could possibly be put on this kind of relationship. Don't get me wrong, I am the first person to admit that I love a good relationship. I think it's hot but I was still waiting for a new refreshing spin on romance novels, and this was it for me. So of course you still had the typical kind of damsel in distress and then that sexy as hell man coming to save her. **Well the twist is something that you wouldn't expect....** Wulf also has a secret, and when I mean secret, it's a big secret. No, it's nothing that you might be thinking, like he is married or he is gay. **I mean huge, I was in complete shock when I found out.** That is one of the things that I loved most about this novel, **everything that I thought was completely wrong and it kept me intrigued the entire time.**" ~*Fictional Book Ho's Blog*

"The writing was great and I loved the way the author "peeled away" the layers of them and let us really get to know them gradually. I loved the mystery in the characters backgrounds and personalities. I loved the suspense and action thrown in the story also!" ~*Sammy's Book Obsession*

ALSO BY BLAIR BABYLON

The Rock Star's Secret Baby (Cadell)

Santa, Baby (Peyton)

All I Want for Christmas (Epilogue)

<u>Billionaires in Disguise: Xan Series</u>

"Alwaysland" (Prequel)

Every Breath You Take

Wild Thing

Lay Your Hands On Me

Nothing Else Matters

"Dream On" and "Keep Dreaming" (Epilogues)

"Small Miracles" (Epilogue)

<u>Runaway Princess Series</u>

Once Upon A Time ~~~ OUAT Audiobook

In Shining Armor ~~~ ISA Audiobook

In A Faraway Land ~~~ IAFL Audiobook

At Midnight ~~~ AM Audiobook

Happily Ever After ~~~ HEA Audiobook

<u>Billionaires in Disguise: Maxence Series</u>

One Night in Monaco ~~~ ONIM Audiobook

Rogue ~~~ Rogue Audiobook

Order ~~~ Order Audiobook

Prince ~~~ Prince Audiobook

Royal ~~~ Royal Audiobook

Reign ~~~ Reign Audiobook

<u>Twisted Billionaires</u>

Twisted Billionaire (Book #1)

Tangled Billionaire (Book #2)

Conning the Billionaire (Book #3)

Tempting the Billionaire (Book #4)

Blaze (Twisted Billionaires #5)

Last Chance, Inc. Billionaires

Under Parr (Book #1)

Match Play (Book #2)

Skins Game (Book #3)

Sand Trap (Book #4)

Shark (Book #5)

Dragon's Den Paranormal Romance

Dragons & Magic

Dragons & Mayhem

Dragons & Fire

TEMPTING THE BILLIONAIRE

ROMANTIC SUSPENSE WITH A TWIST

TWISTED BILLIONAIRES
BOOK 4

BLAIR BABYLON

MALACHITE PUBLISHING LLC

To my readers. I love you all.
And thank you for reading.

"It's easier to fool people than to convince them they have been fooled."

— MARK TWAIN

TEMPTING
THE
BILLIONAIRE

Romantic Suspense with a Twist

USA TODAY BESTSELLING AUTHOR
BLAIR BABYLON

Get notices of new releases,
special discounts, freebies, and
deleted scenes and epilogues

Go to:
http://blairbabylon.com/emailbx
On your favorite browser.

MALACHITE PUBLISHING LLC

CONTENTS

TEMPTING
THE
BILLIONAIRE

Romantic Suspense with a Twist

USA TODAY BESTSELLING AUTHOR
BLAIR BABYLON

1

ESCAPE

KYLIE

TEMPTING
THE
BILLIONAIRE
Romantic Suspense with a Twist

USA TODAY BESTSELLING AUTHOR
BLAIR BABYLON

TEMPTING THE BILLIONAIRE
is the epic conclusion to the
Micah Shine Duet.
Make sure you've read *Conning the Billionaire*
before reading this book.

If Kylie screamed, pedestrians on the sidewalk far below would look up and see her with her arms and legs locked around Micah as he rappelled down the side of a four-story office building in downtown Philadelphia.

Kylie Miller (for that was the name she was using) clung to Micah Shine (for that was the name he had told her, *the liar*) as they dangled four stories above the sidewalk, rappelling down the side of the Philadelphia building.

Chilly autumn wind needled through her clothes.

Her teeth ground together, and her hands cramped. The leather of the harness he wore bit her fingers and palms because she was holding on for her life, even though he'd bound her against his broad chest with a thick strap that was cutting into her waist under her ribcage. The bundles of cash she'd stuffed down her shirt poked between her ribs.

Micah bounced off the wall with his legs and held the rope, controlling their descent.

Kylie shook her head, trying to will or pray herself into any other situation, and buried her face in his strong shoulder.

A wide backpack Micah wore, which held two priceless paintings, bonked the side of her face, bruising her cheekbone.

The thin nylon rope slid through Micah's hands and the clips on his chest and stomach. Kylie was hanging off Micah's side like a sideways backpack as he kicked off the wall.

Micah grinned at her as they fell, swaying slowly in the cutting October breeze. His eyes sparkled blue and teal in the fading sunset.

Micah kissed her as they descended, his mouth slanted over hers. The gentle suction from his soft lips on hers tingled down her stomach and shot nervous energy all the way to Kylie's toes.

He broke it off, a wild excitement lighting up his eyes, and he tilted his head to the side to watch the ground rushing toward them.

She bugged her eyes at him, silently asking, *Oh my God, are you goddamned kidding me?* But he didn't look back at her again.

When Kylie craned her head to see above them, Salvatore Grande had stuck his head out of the broken-out window, a black silhouette against the darkening sky. He pointed down at them.

"Micah," she whispered. "We'd better hurry."

More heads emerged from the window.

Male yelling echoed off the brick building across the narrow street.

Thin arms poked out of the window above, arms that terminated in fists spiky with the barrels of handguns.

Kylie gasped, *"Micah—"*

"Brace."

Kylie flipped her legs toward the sidewalk and flexed her knees.

The ground slammed against the bottoms of her feet, her high-heeled shoes clacking on the cement.

With four skilled clicks, Micah freed them from the rope and she dropped away from him, and then they ran toward the corner of the building.

Gunshots banged through the air behind them.

Brick shards and cement chips peppered the backs of Kylie's legs as they skittered around the corner.

She ran harder, reaching with her feet to lengthen her strides as Micah pulled her after him.

Micah's BMW flashed yellow running lights as they raced toward it.

Kylie yanked the passenger-side door handle and tumbled in.

Micah threw the backpack with the paintings over the front seat into the back of the car and slammed the gearshift into reverse as he closed the driver's side door, peering out the rear window with his arm braced on the back of Kylie's seat.

She looked at the windows of the white building, up to the fourth floor where Salvatore Grande's Mafia office was. "They'll come after us."

"And we'll be gone," Micah said.

He cranked the steering wheel to spin the car in a tight U-turn and sped down the darkening streets of Philadelphia toward the freeway.

DRIVE

MICAH

TEMPTING
THE
BILLIONAIRE
Romantic Suspense with a Twist

USA TODAY BESTSELLING AUTHOR
BLAIR BABYLON

Micah wove the BMW 840i through the traffic on the Philadelphia side streets until they merged onto the freeway, and then he sped like a loosed arrow toward Atlantic City.

Kylie was fidgeting in the passenger's seat, finger-combing her long dark hair and tugging on the ends. "We should keep driving and not stop until we get to Ala-*frickin'*-bama or something. We can just leave everything at the hotel."

Kylie Miller, who was actually *Chiarina Merlino*, dammit.

He should have known. He should have *goddamn known.* Sicilian girls weren't named *Kylie*, and she was obviously Sicilian.

She said, "There's nothing in that hotel room that can't be replaced. We can just drive. Maybe Mississippi. Salvatore would never look for us in Mississippi. I'll bet the pasta there is terrible, though."

"I need my computer," Micah muttered as he swung the wheel and slipped through a space in the traffic.

Kylie reached into her shirt and pulled stacks of cash

out. "What's on your laptop that's so important? You weren't writing an autobiography confessing to all your con jobs, were you?"

Worse. "Of course not. And I'm not a con artist. And it's none of your business."

"Yeah, right, you're not a grifter. You just happen to be *really, really good* at scamming people."

"I'm *not,"* he insisted.

Kylie said, "You don't need that computer. You can buy another one. You've got money out the wazoo."

He shook his head as he dodged an eighteen-wheeler changing lanes and nearly flattening them. "I need *that* computer."

"Well, if you knew you were going to steal two paintings from the Mafia and jump out the window, maybe you should've brought the computer with you *so we could flee."*

"Stealing the paintings wasn't part of the plan," he muttered.

"Really?" she asked. "Because you were *wearing a rappelling harness.* People don't wear rappelling harnesses unless they *plan to rappel* down the side of a building or something."

Micah said, "The *plan* was to lay some seeds of doubt in Salvatore Grande's mind by telling him about how my other supposed client, Vincent Genovese, was collecting art by ripping off all the other Mafia Dons in the Northeast, thus violating the Agreement. I was also supposed to stick a thumb drive in his computer and clone it when he wasn't looking."

"Why didn't you goddamn tell me that beforehand?"

"Because you didn't need to know," he growled through gritting teeth. "You can't give away what you don't know."

"Because you thought I'd rat you out? I'm not a goddamn rat, Micah, or whatever the hell your name is."

"You should talk," he growled.

Kylie flipped her hands in the air, her raven curls bouncing around her face. "So even though it wasn't the plan, now we've got two paintings by Old Masters that we stole from the goddamn Mafia," she said, stabbing her finger in the general direction of the back seat. "What are we going to do with them? Toss them in the Schuylkill River? Sell them on a corner in NYC along with our own watercolors? I ask you, *what the hell are we going to do with two red-hot famous paintings?*"

"I know a guy who can take care of the situation," Micah growled.

"You *know a guy?* Jesus, Mary, and Joseph, if that isn't the most *mobbed-up* sentence I've ever heard in my life—"

"*Stop saying that.* I'm not in anyone's books."

"The fact that you know what *in the books* means is incriminating as hell."

"I'm *not,*" he insisted.

"Then what the hell did you mean with that *Marcu* stuff in Salvatore's office, anyway? That's a Sicilian name. Marcus is an Italian name, but *Marcu* is Sicilian. I said you look Italian, but I never said you looked Sicilian. That's pushing it too far, when you were lying to Salvatore. Why are you pretending to be Sicilian?"

Micah glanced at her but returned his gaze to the road ahead as he flipped the car through holes in the traffic. "Look closer."

"Look at what? You're not Sicilian. And trust me, rice cake, I should know. You're far too blond and way too tall."

"I take after my mother. She was Norwegian."

She batted her eyelashes at him, indicating the most

extreme form of skepticism he'd ever seen in his life. "Yeah, and my mother is one hundred percent Russian, but I don't have blond hair or blue eyes. You do *not* look Sicilian."

Micah drove like Mario Andretti through the traffic. "My father was Sicilian."

"Well, that's close enough for the Mob. But if your father is Sicilian, why is your last name *Shine?* That's not a Sicilian name."

"Neither is *Miller.* It took me a few minutes to figure out who you are after Don Grande called you *Chiarina Merlino* and who *your father* was."

Kylie flopped back in her seat and crossed her arms, staring out the front windshield and not looking at him. "I have no idea what you're talking about."

"Joseph Merlino was executed twelve years ago by the Philly Mob. He was shot through the mouth. It was a message job. His body was dumped in the Schuylkill River, where it was fished out later by the police."

"I goddamn *know* how my father died."

"You didn't tell me who you were."

"You know everything else about me. Why didn't you know about my father?"

"You said he was dead."

"He is."

"Then why the hell are you working for the man who *murdered* your father?"

"I didn't have much choice, did I? My mom ran off and took my little sister four years ago, so I had to drop out of high school so I wouldn't end up on the streets. When you support yourself like I do around here, you're either in with Salvatore Grande or on the outs. My girls and I, we give Salvatore a cut, and then we don't have to worry about him or the police or casino security making trouble for us."

"Protection racket," Micah grumbled.

"That's how it's done in AC."

"That's how it's done everywhere."

"You say things like that, and you say you're Sicilian, and then you say you're *not* a made man. I don't know what to believe about you, *Micah*. Or *Marcu*. What did you say your last name was?"

Micah glared at the dark asphalt in the failing sunlight ahead of the car as he merged onto the highway that would take them to Atlantic City. "Yeah, I'm an enigma."

"An enigma with two stolen paintings in the backseat."

He nodded. "We're going to have to do something about that."

She gestured at the four bricks of hundred-dollar bills on her lap. "This is all the money I have in the world, and I need to get the hell out of Atlantic City and stay out. There's nothing left for me here, anyway. He said he'd go after my sister, but I don't know where she and my mother are, dammit. I have to tell my girls they need to scram, though."

A scowl creased Micah's forehead, and his jaw clenched. "You shouldn't contact anyone in Atlantic City. We'll be gone soon, anyway."

"They're my *team*. I absolutely *will* contact them, and then we'll figure out what they're going to do. We always knew that going in as a team might cause problems if one of us had a falling out with Salvatore Grande, but it was worth the risk. At least, it seemed like it was worth the risk *then*. They're going to goddamn kill me. If they have to run, they'll *hate* me, and they'll have every reason to."

"You don't need them. You've got me," Micah heard himself saying before he'd pondered the wisdom of it.

"I'm not sure I want to stick around you," she said, a sharp bite in her voice.

If this shrimpy, mouthy con artist got out of his car and walked away, flipping him off as she did so, Micah's chest would cave in, and his knees would collapse. He sensed his imminent destruction as much as he could feel the sunset's warmth on the side of his face and its blinding rays on the horizon. His eyes cramped from squinting, and the road meandered southward for a few miles before it settled back to its southeastern route toward Atlantic City, putting the sunset behind them.

He said, "We can grab the things we need from the hotel room and hightail it to Boston. Logan has nonstop flights to San Francisco. I'll buy you whatever else you need when we get to California. Don Grande won't even think of looking for you there."

"I can't do that. Salvatore knows your name is Micah Shine because you used your real name in his office. He'll call people at the airport because it's the transportation business, and then his goons will be on the next plane to San Francisco to whack us. We need to *drive* and get out of town."

"When we get to Cali, we'll pick up a few things from my place in San Francisco, and we'll keep going. We won't stop until we're in Paris or Monaco or London. He won't know where to look for you."

Kylie shook her head while she stared out the front windscreen. "I can't do that, and you don't know this guy. You think other Mob bosses can hold a grudge? *Salvatore Grande* can hold a goddamn grudge like no one else, and we're going to end up dead somewhere. I don't want Rita, Alma, and Priyanka to get whacked, too. It's not fair to take them down with us."

"He's not going to go after your friends. I'll put the word out on the street that I lied to you and used you."

"And you can 'put the word out on the street,' but supposedly, you're not connected with the Mafia. Something doesn't add up with you, *Marcu.*"

"Grande will blame me," Micah said, running over her line of conversation and turning it. "If he got conned by a bunch of small-time con artists, he'll lose face. He won't want people to think that four girls stole his paintings from under his nose and took him for millions of dollars like that. The Mafia is inherently misogynistic."

Kylie snorted. "You've got that right."

"He's going to be looking for someone bigger than you to blame. He's going to be looking for *a man.* I gave him the Genovese Family as a target. Salvatore Grande isn't going to go after you and Alma and Priyanka. He's going to go after Vincent Genovese, and he's going to get his ass kicked."

"Grande is smarter than that, and all those Mafia Dons talk to each other now. They don't go to the mattresses over some rumor," she said.

A chuckle bubbled up Micah's throat at how Kylie —*Chiarina Merlino*—talked. He wasn't the one who used Mafia vernacular in every sentence; she was. *Going to the mattresses* meant a Mafia war between families.

He said, "Vincent Genovese has wanted to take over the Philadelphia and Atlantic City territories for decades. Grande knows it." Micah smiled as he aimed the car down the long highway and pressed the pedal to the metal floor to keep ahead of the goons that Salvatore was doubtless sending after them. "Grande absolutely *will* believe that Genovese would screw with him like that, and both of them will jump at the opportunity to launch an all-out war because they both think they can win."

Kylie still had her arms wound tightly across her chest.

"Was that your plan all along? Get a bunch of made men and their families murdered just for the hell of it?"

Micah's stomach clenched, and a sour taste rose in his throat. "No. It's just the beginning."

"I don't suppose I need to waste my goddamn breath *again* that you need to tell me what your damn plan is."

"What you don't know, you can't divulge. And it's better that you focus on your own goals, anyway. You don't need to be distracted with details about stuff you don't need to know."

Kylie frowned. *"Figures."*

"Don't call them until we're on our way out of town, then," he said. "We need a head start."

"I should—"

He lowered his voice. "Don't."

"Fine," she said, tossing her raven-black curls and looking out the window. "Whatever you say."

The snarl in her voice left no doubt that she would have whacked him if she could have.

CLOSE CALL

KYLIE

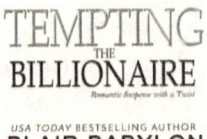

ylie's few clothes in Micah's suite at the Ocean Resort didn't even fill a carry-on roller suitcase.

Micah had been staying at the Ocean Resort for almost two weeks. His suits, hair supplies, and oversized shaving kit required a larger bag.

In the walk-in closet, Kylie clapped his suits together in their dry-cleaning bags, lifted the hangers off the rod, and rolled the rustling plastic around her arms as she dashed back to his suitcase on the luggage rack to stuff them in.

Packing everything else took a few more minutes as she scooped their toiletries off the bathroom counter and into his suitcase lying on the floor.

Kylie trotted out from the bedroom, dragging their luggage across the thick carpeting underfoot.

Micah was on the phone.

The goddamned phone.

Salvatore Grande's goons would be there *any minute* to whack both of them, and Micah Shine was on the *phone.* They needed to *leave.*

Kylie demanded, *"Are we ready?"*

He lowered his phone and grinned that straight-gaze smile at her. "Let's go."

Grabbing the handle of the larger bag away from Kylie, he slung his computer bag over his other shoulder. Kylie held back while Micah opened the door and peered into the hallway.

"Come on," he said.

At the elevator, the doors slid open as soon as he touched the button, and they hurried inside.

The elevator doors hesitated like they were waiting for someone else to get in.

Come on, come on, dammit. Kylie fidgeted with the handle of her suitcase.

The doors leaned out from the sides of the opening, drifting toward each other.

The stairwell door at the far end of the hallway slammed open.

Footsteps thundered, running behind their baggy-suited leader, Tony *frickin' Fava* Bean.

Before Kylie could step back, Micah shoved her toward the elevator wall, out of sight.

The open space between the elevator doors narrowed.

Micah didn't move out of the line of fire. His sinister grin at Salvatore Grande's goons radiated *kill me if you goddamn dare* Mafia energy.

The idiot. He was going to get himself *whacked.*

Kylie stayed plastered to the wall, waiting for Micah's head to explode.

The elevator's door kissed closed, and the floor under their feet shifted, dropping.

"Jesus, Mary, and Joseph, what's the goddamn matter with you?" Kylie yelled at him and backhanded him on his thick

biceps. She slapped his stupid butt and chest for good measure. "They were going to shoot you!"

Micah laughed out loud and curled his leg and arm while recoiling against the side of the elevator as if she'd tickled him. "But with any luck, they'll forget you were in the elevator."

She dropped her hands to her sides but kept her fists clenched. "That doesn't matter! Were they drawing their guns?"

Micah straightened and brushed his hands at his suit jacket, smoothing creases. "Well, yeah, but the elevator doors were closing. It was fine."

"It was not *fine!* You can't go getting yourself killed, you *cafone!*"

Micah glanced down at her from the corners of his eyes. "That almost sounded like you care."

She snarled at him, "You got me into this, Micah Shine, and you're going to get me out of it. Don't go getting yourself whacked before you do it, either."

The elevator doors opened to the parking garage, and they walked out. Their suitcase wheels grated over the cement floor and echoed off the walls, and darkness rose from the ground as night overtook the city.

Micah was goddamn reckless. He was going to get himself killed and take her with him. Hanging around him was a dumbass move.

Kylie veered away from him, walking with long strides toward the exit to the sidewalk.

"What's wrong now?" Micah called after her.

She turned around and yelled at him, "This is *frickin' insane!* You're a lunatic who's trying to start a Mob war! Who even *does* that?"

"It's for a good reason."

That was *it*. She'd had *enough*. To hell with *this guy*.

Kylie pivoted and started walking away from him toward the staircase at the corner of the garage. "And you won't tell me what that reason is."

Micah called after her, "We have a contract for a month."

She strutted away from him. *"So frickin' sue me."*

"Grande's hit squad is doubtless running down the hotel stairwell as we speak and will barge through that very door you're walking toward within minutes."

Dammit.

Kylie made a U-turn and stalked past Micah toward his car, staring straight ahead with her nose in the air. *"Fine. Have it your way."*

At the car, Micah tossed their suitcases in the trunk and then reversed out of the parking space. He didn't slow down until they hit the expressway.

The whole time, Kylie stared straight ahead with her arms tightly crossed over her chest. *The nerve of this guy. The frickin' nerve.*

When they'd been driving on the expressway for a few minutes, she tossed her black curls and said, "I don't know where you think you're going, California or whatever, but I can't go with you. My little sister is out there somewhere, and Salvatore Grande threatened *her* because I was betraying him. I have to find her before he does."

Micah shot a glance at her out of the corners of his eyes and kept driving. "She and your mother left four years ago, and you haven't found them yet. What makes you think you'll find them now?"

"Because I have to," Kylie said, feeling her teeth grind together. "Because they're my family, and family is everything."

4

WE DON'T SLEEP WITH MARKS

KYLIE

The BMW sportscar growled through the night as they drove toward the freeway out of Atlantic City. The grimy haze of light pollution from the casinos and urine-color streetlights drowned all but the brightest stars in the night sky above them.

Micah drove quickly, aggressively, slamming his BMW through the Monopoly-named small streets toward the freeway, but Kylie was accustomed to New Jersey drivers. His driving didn't scare her.

Admitting to Rita, Alma, and Priyanka that she'd screwed things up with Salvatore Grande scared her.

Kylie made the call anyway.

After only half of a ring, Rita answered. "Hello? Kylie? *Are you okay?*"

"I'm fine," Kylie said. "Is everybody else okay?"

The four of them worked together to accommodate Atlantic City tourists who desperately wanted to do something wrong. They were a team, best friends, and four work wives.

Or as the four girls liked to joke, *future co-defendants.*

Rita told her, "Alma and Priyanka are getting ready for tonight. Where the hell are you?"

Beside her in the car, Micah must have overheard her call because he growled, "Don't tell her *anything.*"

Kylie ignored him and told Rita, "I'm leaving town."

"*What?*" Rita yelled into the phone. "We can't work without you. What the hell is going on?"

"I'm really sorry. I had a problem with Salvatore Grande."

"You *what?* What do you mean *you had a problem with Salvatore Grande?*" Rita demanded.

"Don't give her any more information," Micah said. The car accelerated as they took the exit to the Garden State Parkway. "Just hang up. You shouldn't have told her that we're leaving town."

Kylie brushed her hand at him and told Rita, "I'm with that guy I met a while ago at the Borgata casino, Micah Shine."

"Dammit," he muttered.

Rita said in her ear, "Kylie, we've had this conversation. *We don't sleep with marks,* and we *sure as hell* don't go to the second location with them. I *know* that time you slept with him was a one-time thing because he was hot, but you need to *stop this* and *come home.*"

"I'm not going to the second location with him. I need to leave town, and he's leaving, too."

Micah growled, "Stop giving her information."

Kylie wanted to slug him. Instead, she said to Rita, "I made a deal with Micah, remember? I signed a contract with him for a month that will make me a *hell* of a lot of money and give us all a cushion for a while. And he isn't from around here, so Salvatore probably won't know about it. We could keep *all* the money."

Rita's voice was dry as she grumbled, "And let me guess. It all went south. As in, there is no money."

"Sort of," Kylie sighed.

Rita's retort was sharp. *"Shit."*

"I mean, I'm still going to get the money," Kylie tried to reassure her. "You'll still get your cut, and then we'll all have some money in the bank even if I'm not here anymore." She turned to Micah, who scowled as he drove. "Right?"

"Yes," he said. "We have a deal, but that deal was that you obey me *in all things* for a month. *Now hang up the phone.*"

Rita's voice sounded like scraping metal as it came out of the phone's tiny speaker. *"I'm* not the one you have to worry about, Kylie. We *all* have to worry about *Salvatore.* And if everything went south with Salvatore, your Micah Shine guy isn't going to give you any money because he's going to end up in the Schuylkill River."

A fetid wave of sick sweat broke over Kylie. *Bloated corpse, her father, his lower jaw hanging and the back of his head blown off.*

Animal damage.

Rita didn't know about Kylie's dad. No one in her life did.

Except for Salvatore.

And now, somehow, *Micah.*

She said to Rita, "Yeah, well, Salvatore is why we're heading north out of Atlantic City."

Micah growled, *"Stop telling her our location."*

Rita asked, "Are you in the car with him *right now?"*

"Yeah. We're turning off the AC connector onto the Garden State Parkway and heading toward Boston. I think we'll be there tomorrow morning. Probably sooner. The souped-up, midnight blue 840i BMW that he rented is *fast.*

Boston is like, what? Six or seven hours from AC? I think our plan after that is for him to fly to San Francisco and me to get lost on the East Coast somewhere."

Rita screeched, "Jesus, Mary, and Joseph, Kylie! You need to come back and go to Salvatore *on your knees—*"

The phone slipped out of Kylie's hand, leaping upward into Micah's fingers. *"Hey!"*

Micah glanced at her phone while he drove with his other hand and crooked his thumb to power it off. As the screen faded, he tossed it in the back seat. "I *said* to stop talking to her."

"What the hell, dude! *You can't do that!*"

"Oh, yes, I can."

She unclicked her seatbelt. "I'll just reach back there and grab it."

He accelerated, and the engine's growl rose to a whine above the beeping seatbelt alarm. Force shoved her back into her seat. He said, "Sit down and buckle your seatbelt, or I'll throw your phone out the goddamned window."

"She's my friend!"

"And you gave her *far* too much information about our location, the car we're driving, and our plans. Betrayal is *exactly* why I don't tell *anyone* the whole picture. People can't rat you out if they don't know what's going on."

Rage tore through Kylie as she jammed her seatbelt into the buckle. "I didn't *betray* you! I'm *not* a *rat!*"

"You told her *too much.*"

"It probably doesn't even matter. Salvatore probably put AirTags on those paintings and can see where we are on his damn phone."

"Yeah, we'll have to watch on our phones for a notification. But Salvatore Grande will interrogate your friends about where we're going so he can get there faster."

Kylie flipped her hands at him. *"Of course,* he will. That's why I was giving Rita *something to tell him!"*

Micah's aqua-flecked eyes flared as he glanced at her and then at the rearview mirror and started to change lanes. "That wasn't *something.* You were *giving away* our actual location, vehicle, and plans to your friend *so she could tell Salvatore Grande.* Look, if you want to take your chances with the Don Grande, I'll pull over and let you out right here on the Garden State. Or maybe you've been working for him against me all along. Have you?"

Kylie yelled at the stupid goombah driving the car, *"No,* I'm not working *for him, against you!* Rita has been my *family* these last few years. I can't just throw her to Salvatore like, 'So long and good luck, bitch!' He'll break Rita's fingers or kidnap her niece or something to get her to talk. I had to give her *something* so Salvatore would get off her back!"

"You didn't give her *something,"* he growled. "You gave her *our whole plan,* the *car* we're driving, and where we're *going.* That's *everything."*

"And yet, it probably won't be *enough!* I have to keep Rita and my friends *safe.* When Salvatore goes after them for *my* betrayal, it's *my* job to keep them *safe."*

"Rita is *not* your responsibility," he grumbled.

"Yes, she *is.* She's *more* than just my responsibility." Longing crushed her chest. "She's my *family,* or the closest thing I have to one anymore."

"Rita is *not* your *family.* How long have you been working with her?"

"Four years."

"That's nothing."

"It is *not."*

Micah huffed as he drove. "I've been working with a guy for over a decade, and he's *not* my *family."*

"Sounds like a *you* problem," Kylie snarked.

"He was my friend when we were in school, but now he's a *business* contact. Business is separate. Business is *always* separate."

"Yeah, well, I *don't* separate business and friendship. My girls are my *fam*. Just because you have some sort of *trauma* and can't be friends with people you work with doesn't mean it's my problem, too."

"I don't have any goddamn trauma."

"Yeah, *sure* you don't."

"You can't just *trust* people like that in this business, and you mustn't betray me just because you're 'friends' with her."

Kylie could hear the air quotes in Micah's voice, and she flipped him off.

He continued, "Rita is not your responsibility, and she must have known the risks when she got involved with the garbage business."

There it was again: *the gah-bige business,* an insider term for the Mafia, and spoken with a New York accent. "Sounds like you know a lot about *the garbage business,* what with you insisting that you're 'half Sicilian' and all your references to *Vincent Genovese."*

"I have no idea to whom you refer," Micah said, and now his accent was hard-starched British.

"Bullshit," Kylie accused him. "You're a chameleon, aren't you? No matter where you go, you blend in like a chameleon, but bits of the real you keep poking through. I see them."

His sharp glance at her was a flying dagger. "I don't know what you're talking about."

Still with the British accent.

"Sure, you do," she said. "You're one of those guys who's

tough on the street like a *capo dei capi* but then slides right into regular society like butter wouldn't melt in your mouth. When I first met you at the Borgata, I didn't sniff any of the Family on you. You were like this generic guy in AC, just there to get into a little bit of trouble like all the rest. You could have told me that you were a farmer boy from Iowa City, Iowa, at the hotel for a white bread convention, and I would've been all, 'Yeah, that checks out.' But you slip sometimes, like when we were eating at Angeline, that Italian restaurant."

"You're mistaken," he said, and the car accelerated under the sodium streetlamps in the dark New Jersey night.

"Nah, I don't think so. The way you broke the bread with your hands and ate, you're Italian. I could practically see the connections. If you're Sicilian, who are you related to?"

"I beg your pardon?"

"Small island, even if there are big families. After what we did, it would be creepy if we were cousins or something."

He shook his head. "I'm not related to the Merlinos."

So he knew her father's people. "Oh, and so who *are* you related to, then?"

"No one," Micah said, lower, harder.

"Oh, come on. You can't be related to *no one* if you're Sicilian. Even if you're from the other side or your dad was, everyone is related to everybody over here."

"I'm not," he said, his voice chopping like an ax.

Kylie rolled her eyes and held her palms face-out to indicate *hands-off.* "Okay, Mr. Touchy. I'm sorry I asked."

The car sped through the night. Kylie gripped the door handle as Micah accelerated through the turns.

Finally, she said to him, "If we're going to Boston, I can help drive. It's a long way to drive solo."

He growled, "We're not going to Boston anymore, and don't call your friends."

Great. "Where, then?"

He frowned. "I know a guy who lives in the city."

Kylie kept her eyes wide so she wouldn't sprain her eyeballs from rolling them so hard.

Micah *knew a guy.*

In the city.

Shocker.

5

LOGAN BELL

MICAH

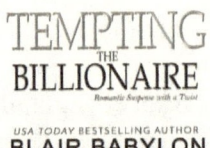

Fourteen years before, four American high school boys had been admitted to the *Institut Le Rosey,* the Swiss boarding school for billionaires on the shores of Lake Geneva, on scholarship as a superficial gesture on the part of the school to appear less outlandishly elitist.

The four of them—Tristan, Logan, Blaze, and Micah—had stuck together.

They'd had to. They say that money can't buy class, and it certainly can't purchase empathy or kindness.

The four scholarship kids had banded together and survived, and they'd thrived in the seven years since graduating.

Micah had been living in a San Francisco penthouse for the last two years, though he'd rarely been there.

Tristan King lived on a yacht in Monaco doing something with computers. Blaze Robinson was a finance guy.

But Logan?

Logan Bell lived in New York City, the bright glow on the nighttime horizon that Micah and Kylie were driving toward, and he didn't talk much about what he did.

Micah had been avoiding the hell out of Logan ever since Micah had received that goddamn letter months before, calling in the debt from when Logan's grandfather had loaned each of the scholarship kids seed money to start their lives.

Because Micah didn't know if Logan was part of the problem.

Micah had been talking to Mary Varvara *Bell,* who had taken over the territory or business or something from Stanley *Bell,* who was Logan *Bell's* grandfather.

And while all those names seemed to intersect, it didn't *feel* right. Mary Varvara Bell had a Russian accent and sensibilities.

Stanley Bell and Logan were definitely a hundred percent Italian.

Maybe MVB had stolen the name along with the crime syndicate. Weirder things had happened in the underworld.

And this would be the first time Micah had seen Logan since he'd received that threatening letter from MVB calling in Micah's debt to Stanley Bell, and that had changed everything.

Micah's life had turned upside down.

As he drove, he turned the corner onto the road skirting the expanse of Central Park and passed an ugly mirrored monolith of a hotel with the doors roped off and a foreclosure sign on a signboard on the sidewalk. *Sweet Baby Jesus Christ on a cracker, how fucking stupid and corrupt does a person have to be to bankrupt a hotel in Midtown Manhattan with a Central Park overlook?*

His car nosed down a ramp into the parking garage under Logan's building, 15 Central Park West.

Micah handed Kylie out of the car and reached into the back seat for his laptop and the wide case with the paintings. He told the valet, "Deliver the rest to twenty-four B," as he dropped the rented BMW's key fob in the man's gloved hand.

The valet closed his hand over the fob. "Mr. Bell expecting you?"

"Certainly," Micah said, keeping his teeth together and his best British accent firmly in place. Americans remembered British accents.

As they rode the elevator from the parking garage, Kylie asked, "Did this guy ever reply to your text?"

"He doesn't have to," Micah said as his ears popped, and the whine of the elevator was suddenly louder.

On the twenty-fourth floor, the doors whooshed open. Micah led to the right and pounded his fist on the single door on that side of the hallway, #24B.

Logan Bell opened the door, his green-eyed gaze an inch above even Micah's, and he said, "Micah, my friend, I've been expecting you to show up here eventually."

His accent was pure New Yorker, so guttural that he sounded like an Italian straight outta Brooklyn.

Micah buried his own native accent more deeply in his brain.

British, he reminded himself. *Round, dark brown vowels. English to his core.* He always used those posh British intonations around Logan, ever since their instructors at *Institut Le Rosey* had insisted the Americans learn to speak English "correctly."

"Yes, quite," Micah agreed, walking into the pristine white foyer while Logan shut and locked the door behind them with a clatter of spinning deadbolts. A round mirror above a glass-topped entryway table reflected the three of them facing off.

Micah said, "May I present my associate, Miss Kylie

Miller. Kylie, this is Logan Bell, an old school chum from back in the day."

"Nice to meet'cha," Kylie told Logan and offered her hand to shake.

Logan smiled down at tiny little Kylie. He grinned with one corner of his mouth and asked her, "How *you* doin'?"

The Le Rosey boarding school was rumored to spike the water with something to make its male students grow so prodigiously, but at six-five, Logan had sprouted an extra inch above everyone else.

Kylie looked far up at Logan, caught Micah's gaze, and then looked back to Logan. Her dark eyes were shadowed with her most unknowable thoughts, and she said to Logan, her voice husky, "Well, *hello there.*"

Absolute violence writhed in Micah's core, the sort that beat men's faces to hamburger if they looked at a woman wrong. The kind that pistol-whipped underlings or pulled the trigger when the barrel was pressed against a man's forehead.

Not rage.

Not shallow revenge.

But a deep wellspring of brutality linked to a need for control in every situation.

Micah rested his hand on Kylie's shoulder and mentioned to Logan, "We've known each other for a bit."

Logan released Kylie's hand and turned to face Micah.

Yeah, Logan should get his filthy fingers off Kylie Miller.

"Where you been?" Logan asked Micah, his New York accent as rough as it always had been outside of an English class.

At first glance, Logan looked like a corn-fed Brahman bull straight from the fields of Nebraska. Powerfully broad across his enormous shoulders, he had a wide skull and cheekbones, and an ivory complexion.

Logan had never displayed the placid patience of Brahman cattle or any domesticated or prey species.

When he stared into Micah's eyes, searching for answers, Logan's bright green eyes held the dangerous intelligence of a predator, a snow tiger or a white wolf, not bovine.

Micah locked his jaw to keep his teeth firmly together as he spoke. "I've a flat in San Francisco for my base of operations these days."

Logan's stare didn't flicker. "That's not what I asked."

"I say, old chap," Micah continued, "we seem to've had a bit of a run-in. Do you mind if we kip here tonight?"

Logan finally broke off and waved vaguely at his wintry apartment, the cream rugs on the herringbone floor, the white couches in the snow-painted living room off to the right. "Yeah, *mi casa es tu casa.* The guest bedroom is at the end of the hall that way." He flipped his hand to indicate the corridor extending from the left side of the foyer. "How long you staying?"

"Just tonight, I should think."

"What's in the funny-looking bag, and where you off to after tonight?"

Micah sighed for theatrical effect. "So many questions, Logan. Can we set down our bags before the third degree?"

"Where are my fucking manners?" Logan said, his New York accent making the obscenity sound more like *fookin'.* "Go on to your room that way. You eat?"

"We stopped at a service area."

"You eat *food?*" Logan asked, clarifying.

Micah's New York accent snuck up on him. "I could eat. You hungry?" he asked Kylie.

She nodded, her ebony curls tumbling over her shoulders.

Logan said, "I can order something to be sent up from building's restaurant. They're usually quick. Set your bags down and come over to living room to look at the menu."

The door at the end of the leftward hallway led to a large bedroom with floor-to-ceiling glass for the back wall, over-looking the sparkling galaxy of nighttime Manhattan.

Micah shut the bedroom door behind them and locked it. He checked the corners of the room with a quick glance. No overt cameras or mics, but that didn't mean anything.

"Wow," Kylie said, standing near the window and looking over the expanse. She was still wearing the black skirt and white blouse from that afternoon when they'd visited Salvatore Grande, and her curvaceous form reflected in the window was simply stunning.

"Yes, this is quite the prime location, isn't it?" Micah asked, placing the large square backpack on the wide bed. The heavy wood sank into the comforter.

She said, "Yeah, I'll say. Was that Central Park I saw out the living room windows in the front?"

"It was, and Logan would love to expound upon the view to you."

"Before we go out there," Kylie said, turning her back on the New York cityscape outside the window, "we should get our story straight."

"Absolutely," Micah said, tilting his head.

She was a dark sprite of a woman, curved in all the right places and wasp-waisted, and it wouldn't have surprised him if she'd sprouted dark chiffon wings and hurled glitter-tinged black magic at him. She did have an uncanny way of convincing people to do what she wanted.

Kylie said, "So, we're here for tonight, but we're going our separate ways tomorrow."

Micah nodded. "Spreading disinformation is an excellent tactic."

"No, I mean, *really*, we should part ways," she said. "Obviously, we had to get out of AC after that stunt we pulled, but you can get on a plane and go wherever you want tomorrow. Probably back to the Left Coast, I'd assume. Or, I don't know, Morocco. I'm going to catch a train out of Grand Central to somewhere south, and then Greyhound buses will take me wherever I can hide out for a few decades until Salvatore Grande gets himself whacked. I can tell my girls to meet me wherever I end up. They can't stay in AC, either. It's too dangerous. We can hit those reservation casinos like they never saw us coming."

A tremor shook Micah's body, but he didn't allow it to reach his skin. Micah trailed his fingertips over the square bag holding the priceless Old Master paintings they'd stolen from Grande. "This again?"

"It seems obvious."

"You don't want to go to California with me."

"Look, I mean, we're finished with what we set out to do. You don't have to pay me as per the contract. We'll just break it."

His fingers scratched the bag's black nylon. "Is that what you want?"

"It's what *you* should want. I was your in with Salvatore Grande. Once you were inside his office, you didn't need me anymore. That was the agreement."

Like a dark fae, she was disappearing, slipping like silk threads through his fingers. "This operation has become more complicated. It will have a higher likelihood of success if we work together on it."

"You don't need me," she said.

"It's complicated. We work well together. Look at how well we riffed off each other in Grande's office. We succeeded in liberating these paintings and escaping from an impossible situation."

"We did manage to get out alive," she said, her head bobbing.

"Indeed, and with these irreplaceable pieces of art."

She strolled across the thick rug underfoot toward him, a sultry sway that might as well have been a stalking panther. "So, you need me."

The concept of *needing someone* was a giant rusty hook under Micah's breastbone, threatening to impale him. "We work well together. It would increase the odds that we both survive and meet our goals."

"So," Kylie said, staring up at him with her fathomless dark eyes, "we have a *connection*."

Micah backpedaled. "We could be good *partners* in this."

She rolled her eyes and walked back over to the window, crossing her arms with her back to him to stare over the city in darkness. *"Whatever."*

He followed and stood behind her, bracing his palms against the cold glass above her head, caging her. The slight warmth of her body permeated through the thin fabric of his shirt, and her flowers and feminine scent brushed his face as he inhaled. "You shouldn't throw away what I'm offering you. There's the money, yes, but it's also an opportunity."

"I'm listening," she said.

"If you get on a bus and end up with your team in some backwater town in the deep South, you'll never find your mother and sister," Micah told her.

Kylie shrugged. "Yeah, well, it's been four years. It's not like I'm following some hot lead from here. I don't even know where to start. It's not like I have connections at the FBI."

"You want connections? I have connections to the rest of the world," he growled near her neck.

She shook her head. "Don't give me false hope. You can't find my mother and sister. They're gone. Salvatore was probably lying when he threatened them because even he doesn't know where they are."

"No?" Micah fished in his trouser pocket and came up with the two USB drives he'd used in Grande's office. He slapped them against the glass at her eye level. "I cloned Salvatore Grande's computer. If he knows where your sister and mother are, chances are that the information is on these drives."

She was staring at their reflection in the glass, looking from the drive to his face and back. "You can find my mother and my sister with that?"

He tucked it back in his pocket and sighed heavily. "Yes. Probably. If it's encrypted, I might require help. I don't like promising what I'm not sure of."

She pursed her lips. "I still can't go with you."

Micah ran his hand up Kylie's waist to the back of her head and seized a fistful of her silken hair. He'd thought he'd argued down all her objections. All the logical ones, anyway. "And why, pray tell, can't you stay with me?"

Her voice sounded strangled, but he hadn't touched her throat yet. "Because my driver's license is fake."

He bent her head to the side and ran his lips up the side of her neck, her throat delicate under his lips, and whispered on her skin, "So?"

She whispered, "I can't get on a plane with a fake driver's license. They'll run it, and I won't exist, and they'll put me in jail for having a fake ID. My whole life is a lie."

He slipped his other arm around her waist and molded her plush body against his. His dick was already stiff as hell, and a thrill shot through him as he crushed her against himself. "Oh, that," Micah said. "I always fly private."

She squinted at their dark reflections in the window. "The TSA checks your ID and does all that crap at the airports."

He slipped his hand down her leg and under the hem of her black skirt, trailing his fingers up her thigh. "Private planes fly out of private terminals. We'll drive up to the plane and walk onto it."

"Wait, there's no security?"

He shook his head again as he slipped his fingers inside her panties, his fingertips warm in the slickness between her folds. "Not in the slightest."

She laid her head back on his chest and groaned, "That can't be safe."

He dragged his fingers over her clit, feeling the nub swell with his strokes.

He murmured, "Probably not," and slipped two fingers inside her, stroking her deeper.

Her body went rigid with each stroke, her back arching. "Damn," she said, almost a whimper. "Rich people get all the perks."

Kylie splayed her hands against the glass and pushed harder on his fingers, almost finding her release.

He withdrew his hand and pushed her face against the chilly glass with his other, still gripping her hair.

She gasped at the shock and then punched the glass, a silent toddler tantrum.

Micah growled in her ear, knowing how frustrated she was, "Rich people *always* get the perks. You can have that orgasm when you're a good girl. Logan will be waiting for us."

6

SHERMAN WILLIAMS WHITE-BOY PALE

MICAH

Micah led the way out of the bedroom and down the hallway to the living room.

Kylie's shoes tapped on the wooden floor behind him as she followed.

Other than the golden wood of the floor peeking around the edges of rugs and vibrant flat squares of the oversized books on the coffee table, the thirty-feet-long living room was swaddled in white or medium gray, a cloud tunnel opening to the view of Central Park at the end of the room.

Even on a chilly October night, the twinkle of skyscrapers on the other side of the park glowed faintly on the golds and crimsons of the ever-changing foliage below.

Logan was standing and looking at the view as they entered, seemingly all legs in his black trousers and green shirt that would definitely match his eyes, the bastard. He gestured at the coffee table, where a bottle of vodka was growing ice next to three small glasses. "You want drink?"

"Surely," Micah said, reaching back into his mind for his British accent again. "Kylie?"

She was grinning at the bottle of Yahontoff vodka on the

table. "Oh, wow, you've got the good stuff. I haven't had a properly chilled shot of vodka in ages. That's the problem going to the bars in Atlantic City, you know. Good Bellinis, but lukewarm vodka."

Logan tipped the bottle to pour shots into the tall shot glasses on the coffee table. "They servin' vodka warm? They should be whacked for such an abomination."

She laughed at him. *"Whacked. Sure."*

The frost rime on the glass that had also been in the freezer chilled Micah's fingers, and they clinked them together.

"To new friends," Logan said, smiling directly into Kylie's eyes.

Micah interrupted him, "And old ones."

"Who are you calling old?" Logan quipped and slammed the shot.

Micah followed suit.

The icy vodka burned as it slithered down Micah's throat.

It was already late, but Logan insisted on playing host. They ordered food from the restaurant in the lobby of the building, which was, as promised, far superior to the fast food from the highway rest stop, and sat around talking while they ate.

Micah was sitting on the couch beside Kylie, relaxing into a half-recline after the meal and several more shots of vodka. He braced his knees on the coffee table to keep himself from sliding further.

"Is that supposed to be art?" Kylie asked Logan, gesturing at the three-by-three grid of canvases above the couch where he sat. All were unbroken flat white.

Logan shrugged, picking at the vegetables on the tray

he'd ordered for the table. "They tell me it is. Micah would know more. He's the art guy."

Kylie turned to him. "Yeah, you are the art guy. That looks like somebody dunked a paint roller in Sherman Williams White-Boy Pale and rolled it on. Tell me why all-white paintings are art."

Micah shrugged and pondered the canvases. "The easy answer is that it's art if the person who created it is an artist. It's art if someone says it's art because they know that the person who created it is an artist. If you're talking about an artist like Robert Ryman, he expressed his art through the paint strokes and the textures of the white-on-white materials, but his paintings aren't flat white like these. In his early ones especially, but even his recent ones, there were textures, tints, framing where the brushstrokes didn't quite reach the darker edge, and visual elements to engage the viewer. Agnes Martin has subtle grids in most of her works and was trying to capture the quality of light in New Mexico, like Georgia O'Keefe. The Impressionists were painting the light in France in the late 1800s and were mocked for it. Impressionist paintings by Manet, Monet, Degas, Renoir, etc. now sell for tens or hundreds of millions of dollars."

Logan grunted a laugh. "Those blank canvases don't look like no water lilies."

Micah gestured to the installation, flicking his fingers. "This is in the style of Robert Rauschenberg, who painted unrelieved white house paint on canvases with a paint roller. Art is always a combination of concept and craft. The *Mona Lisa* is art because Leonardo da Vinci's brush strokes are so fine that they are invisible, and it's art because he painted her with that enigmatic smile of hers that haunts your dreams."

Kylie turned on the couch and listened more closely to

him, spurring Micah to greater heights of rumination about art.

"Rauschenberg's all-white canvases were meant as a work of art that was purely an idea, not execution or craft, and to push back at the excesses of other abstract styles like the vibrant color blocks, the unknowable shapes. Rauschenberg's all-white canvases are a clock in the way they reflect sunlight, a snapshot by the way they mirror the colors of yourself and the people with you in the white paint. If you're sensitive enough to read the subtleties in the reflections and shadows, you would look at them and know how many people were in the room, what time it was, and what the weather was like outside. They were part of the Modernist conversation about art in the 1950s. It's art because of the experience he means you to have, not mere brushstroke craft. To prove his point, Rauschenberg had an apprentice slap a fresh coat of white house paint on them in the 1960s, so they aren't even his roller-brush strokes anymore. The point was to renew the reflectivity and mirrorlike surface because that's where the art is, not in the brushstrokes. Afterward, they were still Rauschenberg's art because his *concept* was still the same." Micah allowed, "Perhaps most importantly, he was the first to have the balls to do it."

Kylie rolled her eyes. "Yeah, okay. *Sure.*"

"Yeah, having the insight and courage to do it was probably a lot of the attraction." Micah rolled his wrist, gesturing to the three-by-three grid nailed to the wall above Logan and his couch. "However, back to this. In 1951, Rauschenberg painted canvas groupings of these conceptual works in six variations: one, two, three, four, five, and seven panels. He didn't make any that were *nine* canvases. Thus, this is not a genuine Rauschenberg. At best, it's derivative. It's most likely just decor. I hope you didn't pay more than a few hundred dollars for the materials and labor."

Logan laughed. "More like a thousand bucks, but that money was for the education and time of the interior designer. I don't want people looking at chairs and shit. I want them looking at my eight-million-dollar view."

"And in that," Micah said, raising a carrot topped with hummus as a toast, "it's an excellent choice and displays good taste and modern sensibilities. That's the true art in this room. Every New Yorker wants that view."

"Now, that's what I was looking for!" Logan roared.

Micah hoped that the building, which was less than twenty years old, had adequate insulation in the walls. You didn't want to be an asshole and disturb the neighbors in the small morning hours when you lived in a New York City apartment.

Logan said, "When I pay someone to put some art on the walls, I don't want my guests to be staring at a fuckin' Picasso with the eyes over here and the arm over there," Logan continued at full voice, flinging his arms around like he lived on a forty-acre farm. "The view of Central Park out there is what's magnificent. *That's* what I paid for. I'm gonna use what you said there, Micah, my friend. 'Every New Yorker wants that view.'"

"It is amazing," Kylie said, sighing at the dim city lights sprinkled on the autumn treetops.

Logan promulgated upon the benefits of the view for minutes while Micah sat with his ankle crossed over his knee and his arms spread on the back of the couch, evaluating every word Logan spoke to determine whether it crossed the line with Kylie.

Not quite.

And Micah was enjoying the view, of course, meaning

his view of *Kylie,* her raven-wing hair and the sparkle in her dark eyes as she listened to Logan natter on. She was probably utilizing her con artist wiles to appear *simply fascinated* by everything Logan said, but Micah was the one enraptured by her smile.

Midnight had been in their rearview mirror for a while, and Kylie stretched and yawned. "It was *great* meeting you, Logan." She turned to Micah, who was more interested in the way her body moved under that tight white shirt she wore than Logan's diatribe about trees. "I'm going to hit the sack."

Micah smiled his most easygoing smile at her, not like he was gloating in front of Logan. "I'll join you soon."

Well, maybe a little.

"Yeah, you go on," Logan said to her. "My friend Micah and I have old school-chum stuff to catch up on."

Micah and Logan did have much to catch up on, but they wouldn't because it was not mere gossip.

The scholarship kids had often spent a day or two at the end of the holidays with Logan and his grandfather, Stanley Bell, because the old man would ferry them between his Manhattan penthouse and JFK Airport to return to their Swiss boarding school.

Stanley Bell had not been a good influence on the four teens. Indeed, Stanley Bell had been in the habit of downing a few bourbons and expounding on his methods of getting ahead in the real world, most of which involved blackmail, bribery, beatings, threats, and the occasional strategic murder.

Micah Shine had sat at the old mafioso's feet and kept his mouth shut tight, pretending to be as shocked as the others when their Malefactor revealed his methods.

He'd wanted to crawl over the thick Persian rugs out of

the apartment and never return, but that would have also invited questions.

After the four scholarship guys had graduated with their college degrees, the Malefactor had offered them interest-free loans with no repayment schedule. The other three guys had barreled into the opportunity.

Only Micah had been hesitant—no, *resistant*—to taking the old *mafioso's* money for no stated purpose.

When his reticence had become more dangerous than the risk of accepting, Micah had caved and grinned while signing the Malefactor's promissory note, lest he crack his cover story.

And then, after the Malefactor's death, Mary Varvara Bell—she of the lilting threats and all-white office decor like a misunderstood Modernist painting or a Moscow winter— had ended up in possession of Micah's contract and his promise. Logan *Bell* had never said a goddamn word to any of them about how *that* had happened.

Discussing it would lead to one of two scenarios in Micah's mind.

One possibility was that Micah would end up shoving Logan against the wall by his throat with a gun pressed under his jaw, telling him that *Micah* didn't have a problem with Mary Varvara Bell, *Logan* did, and Logan had better take care of his fucking problem real damn quick before Micah lost his patience.

That was how Micah's family had handled matters like this all the way back to his Sicilian ancestors on the other side of the ocean.

Alternatively, Micah could keep his damn mouth shut and proceed with the plan he and Arthur Finch-Hatten had hatched years before.

Micah knew how to keep his mouth shut. Omertà was as much of a religious practice as a vow of honor in his family.

Except after they heard Kylie shut the bedroom door down at the other end of the hallway, Logan turned back to Micah and asked, "Who the fuck are you?"

Micah scowled at him and remembered to Briticize his accent before he said, "I say, old chap, have you had a head injury?"

"I've been looking into you, 'Micah Shine.' I would've sworn to Mother Mary that I knew you, but then it turns out, I don't. You may be telling people *now* that you're from Midwest and try to talk like you don't have no accent, but I remember when you *twalked* just like I do. And then when someone said something and I looked into you, it turns out Micah Shine doesn't exist. You weren't born in Nebraska or nowhere else."

This was a problematic turn of events. "I have no idea what you're talking about."

"That was quick, yeah, but you've been practicing that for fourteen years, haven't you? You can learn how to cover up accent real good in fourteen years."

Micah shrugged. "Master Hamilton at Le Rosey took a particular interest in us four scholarship boys, and he beat those American accents right out of us, didn't he? If we hadn't learned to speak 'correctly,' he would have failed any one of us, and we would have lost our scholarships. You can speak with a proper accent, too, when you choose to."

Logan glared at him and then rolled his eyes. When he spoke, he sounded just as British as Micah. "Of course, I can, but I shan't unless I'm with the trust fund babies from *Le Institut.*" His accent reverted to New Yorker. "But you ain't one of them."

"Hamilton's posh English accent took with me, and I trot

it out sometimes. I don't see why the habit deserves that sort of response."

"Because you don't have no papers. Micah Shine wasn't *born* anywhere."

He shrugged. "I don't know where you looked, but evidently, it wasn't in the right place. We got on the same planes to and from Le Rosey every year. I handed over my navy-blue US passport at immigration control, same as you did. Do I have to show you my current passport to prove that I am, indeed, Micah Shine?" He could.

Logan shook his head. "Passports can be forged."

Micah scoffed. "They really can't. They have biometric data and RFID chips connected to the federal government. Perhaps fifty years ago, forging a passport might have been possible with proper artwork. Now it isn't even a believable plot device in a bad spy movie." He flipped his hand at Logan, nearing the end of his patience. "You should know all of this."

"And yet, Micah my friend, why can't I find any trace of you before you walked onto that flight to Le Rosey when we were fourteen?"

Because Micah had been eleven, and he hadn't been Micah Shine. "Absence of evidence is not evidence of absence. The logic instructors at Le Rosey taught us better than that."

"You are falling back upon the logical fallacy of *argumentum ab auctoritate*, arguing to authority, instead of denying it."

"I've already denied it. I can show you my passport yet again, but we were all in Monaco just a few months ago for Maxence's wedding. Logically, I must have had a passport, then."

"You always fly private. Immigration never looks at passports when you fly private."

Hell yeah, they didn't.

Logan continued, asking, "Where were you fucking born, Micah?"

"None of your fucking business."

That was too much. Suspicious.

Micah sat forward, resting his arms on his knees, and stared directly into Logan's gem-green eyes. "Logan, you've known me since we were fourteen years old. Are you suggesting a con so long that its inception was before we learned to shave?"

With that, Logan's gaze drifted up to the ceiling as he considered it. "That seems unlikely."

"What would I even want from you, other than an occasional spare bedroom and shot of vodka? There's no way I would have known back then that after eight years of knowing you, your grandfather would have offered us a loan that we never had to pay back. He wasn't rumored to be the kindly, generous type."

Micah examined Logan as he said that, watching for any flinch, any flicker of knowledge, but Logan seemed to be reliving their glory days under his grandfather's tutelage. "That's true."

Was Mary Varvara Bell pressuring Logan as well? She might have roped him into her plan to expand her syndicate.

Her scheme might extend farther than Micah or even Arthur Finch-Hatten had suspected.

"What the hell is this really about, Logan?" Micah leaned farther, pinning Logan to the couch with his glare. "Tell me, *old chum,* why the hell were you looking into my goddamn birth certificate after us knowing each other over half our lives? *Something's not right.*"

That caught Logan's attention. He shrugged. "It was just a hunch."

"A *hunch?* That utter drivel is what people say when they are privy to information they shouldn't have access to. 'It was a hunch.' 'It came to me in a dream.' Bullshit, Logan. What the hell is going on?"

At that, Logan sighed heavily and hung his head. "A person in my organization turned out to be a rat. I don't mean she was squealing to the feds. She was in my *finances,* and she was skimming from *me.* I hired her because I'd known her at Le Rosey. Ji-Ho Park, you remember her? She was two years behind us. I'd known her for *years.* I think I fucked her once or twice. She needed a job when her family lost everything in the last real estate crash. Shockingly, she turned out to be just another spoiled, entitled, formerly rich kid who thought she deserved more of my money than what she wanted to work for, so she just took it. It shook me up. What else didn't I know, huh? So, I started looking into things, and something about you didn't add up."

"I am exactly what I appear to be," Micah lied. "You're just a shit researcher."

"I *hired* shit researcher," Logan clarified.

"Whatever."

"So maybe I got paranoid and there's nothing. I'll get that bottle of Yahontoff vodka outta the freezer, and we'll drink to no hard feelings."

"I'll drink to that." The icy vodka might cool the hot sweat prickling Micah's scalp.

Two shots later, Micah stumbled into Logan's spare bedroom, where Kylie was a curvy lump under the blankets in the dark.

Using the flashlight of his cell phone, he found his

pajamas from the jumble of clothes in his suitcase and sat on the bed to stare at the cityscape outside the window. Logan's apartment occupied half the floor of the building, and this second bedroom on the back side of the building overlooked the city instead of Central Park.

The view really was worth eight million dollars.

From the other side of the bed, Kylie's husky little voice asked, "Why is Logan talking like he's trying to be Sicilian?"

Micah plumped his pillow and slid his legs under the covers. "That's just a stereotypical Brooklyn and Manhattan mix."

"There is no way he's really from New York or New Jersey," she muttered. "He's laying the accent on too thick."

Micah shook his head in the dark. "Logan is from New York. Born and raised. His grandfather lived here and ran this town for decades. I met him. Several times."

"But *he's* not," she insisted.

Micah turned. His head spun with the discombobulation of being on the other side of this argument and from the vodka. Probably mostly from the vodka. "I should know where one of my best friends is from. I've known him half my life. I met him when I was eleven," he said, forgetting to correct his age. *"He's from New York."*

"Nah," Kylie said with a yawn as she snuggled under the covers. "He's laying that accent on so thick because he's trying to cover up his Russian accent."

"Logan doesn't have a Russian accent," Micah said, leaning over her slight form with his hands on the mattress between them.

"Sure, he does. It's hard to hear it underneath because he's trying to 'twalk like a Nee-ew Yawker,' but you can hear it in how hard he hits his R's. And sometimes he drops words when he's talking, especially *a* or *an*. And when he says a *th* sound, it almost sounds like a Z half the time."

"He *can't* be," Micah insisted.

"Well, he is. It's funny how a Russian accent sounds so sinister. They can say the most innocuous thing, like," her voice dropped to a deep, ominous tone, *"fuzzy little kitten is playing with mouse,'* and it sounds like a death threat."

Micah chuckled. She mimicked a Russian accent surprisingly well. She could have been one of the Butorin bratva kids at Le Rosey. "I met Logan's grandfather Stanley Bell *often.* He was a straight-up Italian wiseguy. I'm surprised you didn't know him."

Kylie made a sound in her throat like she was going to spit a hairball. "Bah, you met *one* of his grandparents. Logan had three other ones, the standard number. He's as pale as you, rice cake, and you're *supposedly* half Sicilian. I'll bet he's half-Russian or more. Maybe three-quarters. And he grew up at least part of his childhood there. Probably Moscow, although Russian accents are pretty homogeneous."

"Huh," Micah said, and a thousand connections sparked in his brain like a branched lightning bolt. "Yeah, I'll have to ask him about that."

He really would have to.

Just as soon as the bedroom stopped spinning.

7

TALKING TO LOGAN

KYLIE

The following day, Kylie dragged her slightly hungover butt out of bed.

Micah was sleeping like an angel—an enormous, muscle-bound, curly-headed angel wearing a plain black tee shirt and jammie pants and breathing so softly she almost held a mirror up to his nose until he sighed. One giant foot was sticking out from under the covers. His toenails were clean and trimmed, and none had toenail fungus.

Hygiene said a lot about a person in Kylie's experience. Guys with blunt, filed fingernails bought the best jewelry, while guys who smelled like expensive cologne and cigarette smoke were more likely to lose track of how much gambling money they'd given her and keep pouring it on.

Guys wearing cheap suits and stinky cologne who didn't think they were worth nice things wouldn't think she was, either.

A girl had to know these things.

Kylie did the necessaries for her own hygiene because

girls who don't shower don't attract many marks, and then she wandered out down the long hallway to the other side of the apartment and its spectacular view of Central Park.

Logan was sitting at the small dining table between the living room and the large-for-the-City galley kitchen, drinking coffee and reading on a tablet.

"Any more coffee?" she asked.

He gestured toward the kitchen. "Full pot. Help yourself."

"Thanks." She found a few more cups in an overhead cabinet and filled one.

Logan asked without looking up, "Micah up yet?"

"He's still asleep. How many more shots did you guys do last night?"

"Not enough." He laid the tablet on the table. In the sunshine slanting in the wall of windows, Kylie saw the masthead for the *New York Times*. Logan said, "We need to get him up. You two have to leave."

His jocular spirit from the previous night must have evaporated in the cold fall morning and autumn colors of Central Park outside.

She sipped the bitter coffee. "Why, you got a woman coming over?"

He looked straight at her and leaned back in his chair, crossing his arms. "I don't know who is going to drop in today. Might be very interesting couple of days, considering the trouble you made in Philadelphia last night that you didn't mention. Tell me, what is in big, boxy-looking backpack Micah has brought with you?"

How on Sweet Baby Jesus's green Earth did Micah not hear the flatness of Logan's menacing Russian accent?

Maybe Kylie was just oversensitive to accents, having grown up in a multilingual household.

She said, "Nothing in particular."

Logan rolled his emerald-green eyes and stood, dropping his hands to hang loose at his sides like he might go for a weapon. By standing up from the small table, he'd boxed her in the kitchen, a cabinet-lined hallway with no other exit. He said, "Don't tell lies like that."

"I don't know what you're talking about."

He was still staring straight at her. "What car you drive from AC last night?"

Kylie did not know how she'd thought his eyes were pretty the night before or like anything except dangerous shards of brittle green glass. "A dark blue BMW 840i. Micah said it's a rental."

He nodded. "Go make Micah ready to leave. I'll have you driven to airport and get rid of car for you."

Kylie's head started to buzz, and her nose felt stuffed up like a sinus headache was beginning. "What's going on?"

"Micah will take care of it. You get him up."

Now *that* was the misogyny of the Sicilian Mafia showing through. *Don't you worry your pretty little head about it. Go to the kitchen and make me some veal scallopini, and maybe I'll get you pregnant later.* "I need to know what's going on."

"Nah, you don't wanna know. Get Micah."

Logan sat down at the café-sized table and pointedly picked up his tablet to read his paper again.

Kylie wanted to slug him because, dammit, this guy was obviously *connected* and chauvinistic as hell, but she also knew a losing battle when she saw it.

She also knew problems in the "garbage business" when she saw them, so she went back to the bedroom to wake Micah up so they could get the hell out before they ended up at the bottom of the East River.

Because dead people always ended up in a goddamn river.

8

AUNT MARY

MICAH

Micah strode into Logan's white-swaddled living room and found him drinking coffee at his breakfast table. "What the hell did you say to Kylie?"

Outside the floor-to-ceiling windows, the sun had broken the horizon over the city, and the bright rays slanted into Central Park.

Logan set his coffee cup on its saucer, gently letting it touch down without rattling.

Yeah, he was pissed about something.

Logan said, "You need to get out of here. Out of my apartment, out of New York, preferably out of United States. What the fuck happened with you yesterday?"

Micah summed up Salvatore Grande, Kylie's previous employment, and his liberation of *The Battle of Anghiari* by Leonardo da Vinci in twenty seconds.

Logan didn't blink the whole time Micah spoke. Finally, he said, "So if you're an art thief these days, I guess it's just as well that those canvases in my living room are just 'decor' and not genuine Rauschen-whatevers."

Micah flipped his hand at Logan, flicking away his accusation. "I'm not an art thief. I was liberating one of humanity's greatest treasures from a mafia boss who was hastening its destruction by not keeping it in a temperature- and humidity-controlled environment and was *smoking* right in front of it. I could *smell* the stale cigarette smoke in that office."

Logan shrugged, the philistine. "Right, so that definitely gives you permission to steal it and start a goddamn Mob war, Micah. Ten people are already dead as of this morning. Four from the Philly Mob, six Genovese here in the city."

"Is Salvatore Grande one of them?"

"No."

Good. "That's too bad."

"But ten other good men are."

"Damn, that started fast."

"These things fuckin' do," Logan spat at him.

"Speaking of how things happen too damn fast, who is *Mary Varvara Bell?*"

Logan's expression locked down to solid stone except for a squint of anger at the corners of his eyes. "Who?"

Micah hadn't meant to demand that, but sometimes the Norwegian ice water in his veins gave way to an impetuous Sicilian temper he didn't remember until it was too late. It happened more often than he'd like to admit, like when he saw a goddamn da Vinci on the wall in an office that reeked of cigarettes. "Mary Varvara Bell. She took over *the garbage business* for your grandfather after he died, including our promissory notes from the loans he gave us after we graduated from college. Did you get a letter calling in that loan, Logan, or was it just me?"

Logan's chin dropped, though his expression didn't change. "Your note got called in?"

There was Micah's answer. "Yeah. Now, who is she?"

Logan turned his head and stared for a second over the treetops of Central Park below them, shifting his weight to one leg. That unease could be intentional evasion or surprise, and Micah didn't know which. Logan said, "Mary Varvara Bell is my aunt, Stanley Bell's oldest daughter. She was passed over when he was distributing power when he retired because she was a woman. I heard she didn't take too kindly to that. Maybe she's taking over."

Maybe, huh?

Information about logistics and power was what Micah needed. "Was your father one of the Malefactor's heirs, Logan?"

Logan shuffled his feet. "Never. He and my grandfather never spoke to each other again, and I sure as hell never told my father about the Malefactor's deal. I didn't want to get disowned like his father did to him."

"But *you*, Logan, your grandfather saw something in *you* that he didn't see in his own son," Micah pushed.

His expression changed, becoming angry. "I took the loan, same as you, and I built my companies without *the waste management business* lending a hand. I'm not *connected*, and I'm not beholden to them. I would say, 'same as you,' but *you* were in with the Philly Mob. What the fuck were you doing in *Salvatore Grande's* office when you stole this goddamn painting of his?"

Micah shrugged. "Getting Kylie out from under his thumb," he lied.

"You don't get people *out*. Didn't my grandfather teach you nothin'? Once you're in, no one gets *out*. You guys need to leave. Leave this house, leave the state, leave the goddamn country. I never saw you two. I'll take care of that rental car of yours. You go to La Guardia or JFK, whatever you want."

"JFK," Micah said.

"Don't tell me where you're going."

Micah nodded.

"Go get your shit together, and I never fucking saw you, Micah my friend, or whatever your goddamn name is."

9

GETTING OUT OF NYC

KYLIE

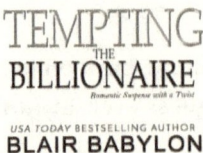

Kylie was on a four-way video call with Rita, Priyanka, and Alma, reassuring them that she was alive and definitely not kidnapped, while Micah was doing a chauvinism with Logan in the living room. "So we're in New York City, staying with a guy who Micah knows. I don't know what his name is. He didn't seem like the kind of guy where you have to know his name, if you know what I mean."

The three of them knew what she meant.

Alma asked, "What's it like in New York City? I've never been."

"Jeez, you've never been to the city for a show?" Priyanka asked her, aghast.

Alma shrugged. "We have shows in Atlantic City. Why would I go all the way up there? Kylie, show us the view."

With one screenshot of the view, someone could triangulate the building and probably the floor they were on.

Rita said, "Yeah, show us the view."

Showing them Central Park, the view from the front side

of the building, would narrow down their location way too much. The sunrise would pinpoint where East was, and the angle of the park would give everything away.

Instead, Kylie padded over to the window there in the back bedroom and held her phone up to the cityscape view, jiggling it a little.

Her phone emitted a chorus of voices. "Hold it still so we can see!"

Kylie turned the phone back on herself and walked back to the bed. "Sorry, I guess even my *arms* are tired after last night."

Jeering hooted from the speaker.

Rita asked, "Did he make you do all the work? Jeez, do guys ever get on top voluntarily?"

Just as Kylie was formulating a saucy response, Micah stormed into the room. "Let's go."

The girls' voices squawked from her phone.

"*What's going on?*"

"*Who's that?*"

"*Where are you anyway?*"

"Mute," Micah said.

Kylie scrambled for the button. "What happened?"

"We're leaving. Get ready."

"Where are we going?" she asked because the phone was muted and she wanted to know.

He said, "Unmute the phone."

She did.

Micah projected his voice more than usual, saying, "We're leaving in five minutes. Our host found out what happened in Philly and is calling the Genovese Family, the feds, or both in five minutes. We need to move the car before we get a parking ticket, anyway. We'll drive to a hotel over in Rockland County or Westchester, maybe one with a parking lot this time. We can hole up there until we figure out where is safe for us to go."

More panic buffeted Kylie, but she noticed that Micah hadn't said Logan's name. "I thought you said you could trust this guy."

"He doesn't owe any loyalty to me. I'm just some guy from his distant past who showed up out of nowhere, asking for booze and a bed for the night. As soon as it seems safe, I'll get myself lost in Chicago or California. San Diego has better weather this time of year. Tomorrow morning, I'll put you on a bus to Alabama like you wanted."

Like she wanted? That wasn't right. "Okay?"

Micah continued, "Let's go. Hey, is that thing still on?"

He grabbed it out of her hands.

Kylie gasped, "Hey!"

Micah powered off her phone and shoved it into the side pocket of the boxy backpack holding the art.

"What the hell!" she demanded. "Is that the actual plan now? Are you going to San Diego and putting me on a bus to Alabama?"

"Of course not," he scoffed.

"But they'll tell Salvatore what we just said! They'll give him *wrong* information, and then he'll beat the hell out of them *or worse!*"

Micah shook his head. "No source is correct a hundred percent of the time. If they were, *that* would be a huge red flag something was too good. They've given him several concrete pieces of accurate information, and now they'll be wrong for once. He won't hurt them, not when they have an inside line to us."

"I can't leave them like this! I need to go back."

He spun and glared at her, his eyes glittering in the morning sunshine like diamonds. "I wasn't kidding. Get dressed. Zip your bag. We need to leave *now*."

Kylie flipped her PJs off and grabbed a dress with a floaty skirt out of her suitcase. It wasn't warm enough, but it was what she had with her.

Logan didn't see them out. They hustled down to the parking garage.

A different attendant stood in the kiosk near the elevators, and she called out, "Are you Mr. Bell's guests?"

"Yes," Micah answered, shoving the handle of his suitcase down. Kylie followed suit.

The parking valet stuck two fingers in her mouth and blasted a piercing whistle through the garage that echoed off the concrete and car metal in the dark corners of the garage.

A limousine with blacked-out windows coasted to a stop in front of them. The chauffeur trotted around to put their bags in the yawning trunk.

Micah opened the door. "Get in."

"This isn't—" she started.

"I know."

Kylie dove into the car and scooted across the velvety leather to sit behind the driver. Her knee-length white skirt trailed across the dark leather seat as she shuffled, and she stuffed it under her thighs to get it out of Micah's way.

Micah stepped into the car after her, his long legs clad in Levi's. His jeans had a knife-edge crease where they'd been pressed, and the dark denim hugged his ass and thighs so snugly that they must have been tailored.

"Where are we—" she began.

The chauffeur wedged herself into the driver's seat and wrenched herself around to ask Micah, "JFK Airport, right?"

"Liberty International in Newark, Signature Flight Support terminal," Micah told the chauffeur. "And hurry. Our flight leaves in an hour."

10

FRIENDS WITH AIRPLANES

KYLIE

A s the car slipped through traffic, questions from Kylie earned her a squinty stare from Micah. She stopped probing.

Weekday traffic was heavy as usual in Midtown, but once they survived the descent into the ceramic-tiled Lincoln Tunnel under the Hudson River and emerged to swerve onto I-95, the half-hour drive into New Jersey was merely dodging speeding drivers.

Kylie said to Micah, "I told you I have a *problem* with getting on a plane."

More death stares, and then Micah resumed looking at his phone.

Kylie didn't *have* her phone because Micah had confiscated it, so she watched the cars around them nearly crash into each other for a while.

When the oppressive silence in the car hung too heavily, she asked Micah, "If my lack of ID isn't a problem, then are we *not* getting on a plane? Are we going somewhere else? Or are you just kicking me to the curb at the airport?"

More hairy eyeball from the grumpy hottie.

"Jeez, a girl would just like to know where she's going," Kylie said, rolling her eyes.

He finally ground out, "We're going to the Signature Flight Support terminal at Liberty International Airport."

"Well, I know *that*," Kylie said. She'd been paying attention when he'd talked to the chauffeur. "But are we going to move in and live there, or are we going somewhere else?"

"You'll know when you need to," he said, with almost a snarl.

"Oh, Jesus, Mary, and Joseph, *this again?* I thought you were going to tell me things and treat me as an equal partner—"

"I never promised that," he snapped. "Compartmentalizing information is important for operational security—"

"Like I *care* about operational security! I just want to know where the hell I'm going!"

"When it's the appropriate time—"

"I've got your *appropriate time* right here, buddy." She squeezed her right boob at him. "And I've got your *operational security* over here, too," she said as she reached for her left.

"And we're here," the chauffeur shouted over their bickering. *"We have arrived."*

"But the terminals are way over there," Kylie said, pointing at the buildings hulking in the distance and the shark fins of airplane tails swimming above them. Kylie knew what the terminals at EWR looked like. Did these Bennies think they could pull one over on a Jersey girl?

Micah opened his car door. "This is the Signature Flight Support terminal for *private* planes."

"But I—"

"Not here," Micah said in a low voice that sent chills down Kylie's spine. *"Get out of the car."*

The low-slung building was midcentury modern with flat roofs and square angles, granite and glass, yet it was unmistakably new. The corners of the stone were sharp, not weathered, and the glass was unscratched.

Luggage handlers trotted out from the larger part of the building, pushing carts toward the trunk. One yelled, "Name?"

Micah took Kylie's arm and steered her toward the terminal, calling back, "Micah Shine."

Kylie had never flown before, but all the TV shows and movies she'd seen had shown jostling crowds pulling luggage in long lines waiting to get to customer service desks.

This building had none of that. Inside, the back wall was glass from the thickly carpeted floor to the second-story ceiling, allowing the autumn morning sunlight to perfuse the entire space. Some people lounged in oversized chairs, watching three enormous televisions set into a wood-paneled wall, and baristas whispered behind an espresso bar at the far end of the building. A few people sat at café tables, sipping their drinks.

Kylie teetered on her stiletto heels behind Micah as he walked up to a long desk on one side of the building and told the guy behind it his name.

The customer service guy wearing a burgundy-and-navy blue uniform checked his computer. "Your plane is ready, Mr. Shine. You can board at your leisure. Your luggage will be stowed within the next five minutes."

This luxurious space seemed right out of the 1950s heyday of flying when people wore suits or cocktail dresses when they traveled on a plane. Kylie spun in a circle, gawking.

Micah took her hand and tugged gently as he steered

her through the glass rear doors and onto the tarmac toward a waiting row of airplanes. Chilly October wind permeated her white dress as soon as they walked into the wide-open space behind the building, freezing her skin and making her break out in goosebumps.

Kylie rocked back on her high-heeled pumps and stopped dead, bracing herself so that Micah didn't pull her off balance. "I need to know *right now* where the hell we're going."

Micah seemed to grit his teeth as he bent and whispered, "On a plane."

"I ain't got a valid driver's license! I ain't got ID!"

He whispered, "I've got you covered. You'll be fine."

"How in the hell are you going to fix me *not having a driver's license?*"

"I know a guy."

Kylie threw her hands in the air in the most exasperated exasperation she had ever exasperated. "I swear to *God,* Micah Shine, if you tell me *you know a guy* one more time, I'm going to start calling you *Vinnie the Bull!*"

He sighed. "I swear to God, I am not in the Mafia. Get on the plane."

"Are we going to Mississippi or California?"

"London," he grated out.

"London? Like the one in *England?* I am *not* going to let you strand me in some foreign country where I don't even speak the language and have no way to get home!"

He squinted at her. "It's in the United Kingdom. They speak English."

"Not if they speak it like you do when you're being all high and mighty. I can't understand half of what you say when you talk like that. And besides, I can't go anywhere without finding my sister and my mother. What am I going to do about that?"

Micah nodded. "A friend of mine in London can help with the thumb drive. If there's any information on it, we'll know, and soon."

This was all highly improbable. Kylie didn't like it when things were too neat. "How do I know you aren't just making stuff up?"

Micah sighed and reached into his back pocket, palming his phone. "How much?"

"I beg your pardon!"

"This always ends with me reminding you of our contract or transferring money into your account. What's it going to take to get you on the plane?"

"God, you are just so *annoying* sometimes. I don't want your *money.* I want to be an equal partner in this business, which means *knowing where we are going."*

"I told you. We're going to Heathrow Airport, London, England."

They were squared off at this point, arguing beside the row of private jets. "Yeah, but you didn't tell me *before."*

"I couldn't tell you in front of the chauffeur or in Logan's apartment. I assumed it was bugged, either by him or the FBI or both. I didn't want *Logan* to know."

"You could've found a way to tell *me."*

"I didn't want *you* to know our destination, okay? You would've told Rita and those other girls, who are a direct conduit to Salvatore Grande."

Propwash or the wind tossed the hem of Kylie's skirt in the air, and she grabbed the material, pushing it down before she flashed her panties at the airport. "If you don't trust me not to tell them, then I shouldn't be on this trip at all. I don't know why you're dragging me around with you if you don't trust me."

"I *wish* I could trust you," he said, and a flash of real emotion laced his voice as the cold wind whistled between the planes. "I *wish* I knew that you were on my side and that you won't tell those girls or Salvatore Grande himself."

Kylie wanted to throttle him and see those pretty, glittery eyes of his bug out. "I have an obligation to keep them safe, but I'm not going to rat you out. Salvatore Grande doesn't have surveillance drones hovering over Manhattan like he's the goddamn Homeland Security. Yeah, I gave Grande *specific* information through my girls, but I didn't give him *important* pieces of information that would have allowed him to actually find us. I'm *not* a rat. If you can't trust me to not give him the *important* pieces of information, I should just *leave.*"

"I don't want you to leave," he said, his voice quieter.

"Why would you want me to stick around if you can't even *trust* me?"

Micah ran his hand through his dark blond hair, releasing the curls. "Because I *like* you, okay? I keep hoping at some point I *will* be able to trust you, that we will be able to work together because we work together *great.* I keep hoping we will be a team and that I can trust you won't betray me and leave me dead on the living room floor in a pile of bodies."

Kylie gaped at him. "That's awfully specific imagery."

He looked toward the line of private planes. "Probably been watching too many movies."

Warring anxieties flooded Kylie's mind and shook her all the way down to her toes. She stamped her feet, undecided whether to run or stomp her stiletto high-heeled into

Micah's foot. "Well, you need to tell me these things. And just for the record, Mr. High and Mighty, I like you, too."

A smile lifted one side of his mouth. "You do, huh?"

"Don't push it."

"And I wanted London to be a surprise," he said, running his hand through his hair again, his dirty blond curls springing free of whatever pomade he used and flipping down over his forehead. "I wanted to show you the UK, take you to the best restaurants, maybe see a show or go somewhere to dance."

"Oh." That changed things. "Well, *why didn't you say so?"*

She swished past him, striding toward the airplanes. "How do you know which plane is yours?"

Micah walked with her and tucked her hand under his arm. "Because I talked to my friend yesterday after everything went south with Don Grande, and he had it flown here overnight."

"'My friend.' 'I know a guy.' Micah, you're a stereotypical Sicilian wiseguy. I wish I had friends like yours with airplanes."

A grimness settled over Micah as they walked toward one of the larger planes, a slim silver jet with a grayed federal-blue tail and a stack of three golden crowns emblazoned on it. "No, you don't."

11

FLYING WITHOUT A PASSPORT

MICAH

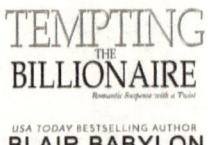

Inside the airplane, eight recliners upholstered in a white leather so fine that it seemed to be fashioned from unicorn hide were stationed two abreast under the row of porthole windows. The other side of the plane held a long couch set against the curving wall.

Micah had never been aboard Lord Arthur Finch-Hatten's private aircraft before. Considering their current relationship and the business they were in, if they hadn't been friends at school, Micah probably wouldn't know Arthur's name.

Not to mention knowing about Arthur's earldom or his vast wealth rivaling any royal family.

But Micah had known all these things about Arthur as simple matters of fact, as much as he'd known that Arthur's friend Casimir had undergone the last of what was rumored to be many facial plastic surgeries during those years, or that Princess Flicka von Hannover was a world-class pianist, or that the Butorin bratva kids shouldn't be messed with if you wanted to come back from vacations with all your teeth or your life.

Then again, if Micah hadn't known Arthur during high school, Arthur wouldn't have sought him out a few years later with a most interesting proposal.

Behind them, the air hostess slammed the airplane door with a hard thunk. Over the intercom, the pilot said, "Stand by for taxiing to the runway."

"That was quick," Kylie said as she sat down in a recliner with a flourish, dropping her purse on a table that had been pulled out between four of the chairs. "I thought flying meant waiting around."

Micah shrugged. "Part of the point of flying private is that you walk from your car onto the plane, and the plane takes off. You should reach your destination for short flights before commercial passengers even board their jumbo jet."

Attending the billionaire boarding school Le Rosey had left him with a lot of life lessons.

"That doesn't seem fair," she said, staring out the porthole window as the plane lurched and began to inch forward.

"That's capitalism," Micah said. "People with money, no matter how they got it, aren't subject to the same rules as everyone else. For example, you noticed that we didn't go through a security checkpoint, and no one asked you for a passport on this end?"

"Yeah," she said, turning to look up at him. Her dark curls framed her elfin face.

"There was no security. Even on international flights, it's the responsibility of plane owners or renters to ensure that everyone aboard has legal permission to leave the departing country and enter the destination country, including whether someone has a passport or visa or is on the American Homeland Security no-fly list."

Her chin dropped as she looked up at him. "That's creepy."

"That's unregulated late-stage capitalism," Micah agreed. "With enough money, even terrorists can fly."

The butler on the plane, who'd introduced himself as "Fothergill, just Fothergill, sir," had cast a wry glance and half an eyeroll in their direction when Micah said that, but he busied himself pouring champagne for day-drinking on the private, intercontinental jet.

Kylie flipped her fingers, gesturing to the reclining seat she was sitting in. "Is this seat okay for me to sit in?"

Micah laughed. "Any seat is fine. You could lay on the floor for the whole trip, though the seats should lie flat into twin-size beds. There are probably sheets and blankets around here if you want to sleep."

"It's ten in the morning. I feel like I just got up."

The pilot announced over the speakers, "Please be seated for takeoff."

Kylie twisted in her chair, looking beside her hips.

"Something wrong?" Micah asked.

"You're supposed to put on your seatbelt." Her knuckles were white, and she gripped the edge of the table. Maybe he should dig around in the corners of her seat and find that belt to make her more comfortable. She said, "First, the air hostess does the two-finger pointing thing, and then they get fascist about seat belts, right?"

"Nah," Micah said, lowering himself into the seat across from her. "That's on commercial flights. You can walk around this plane any time you want. Heck, you can sit in the cockpit with the pilot during the flight if you want to. I mean, you might want to *once*. Private pilots will talk your ear off. Some private planes have bathrooms with showers and full bedrooms."

The engines on the wings outside the portholes screamed, and the plane accelerated, pushing Micah forward in his seat because he was facing the back of the plane.

Kylie snickered. "A bedroom, so people can join the mile-high club?"

He chuckled. "I wouldn't know."

The growl under the plane's tires silenced as the jet levitated into the air above the runway, though the shriek of the engines intensified.

"But this plane doesn't have a bedroom?" she asked.

He leaned over the arm of his chair and looked down the long tube of the plane, but the fuselage ended in a galley kitchen. "Doesn't look like it."

"Want to join the club anyway?" she asked him.

Micah straightened and pressed his palms to the tabletop between them. "Right here?"

Kylie smirked at him. "We wouldn't want to give Fothergill a heart attack. Is there a bathroom on this thing?"

Considering Arthur Finch-Hatten's pre-marriage reputation, Micah doubted Fothergill would be shocked at anything. Nevertheless, he said, "In the back of the plane."

The pilot said over the intercom, "Please remain seated until we reach cruising altitude in about twenty minutes."

Kylie grinned at him. "Just as soon as this thing levels out. I wouldn't want to break something *of yours.*"

Micah clenched his fists and vowed to survive the longest twenty minutes of his life.

It didn't help that the little minx was flirting with him across the table, her naked toe sliding up his ankle and the hem of his jeans.

12

MILE-HIGH CLUB

KYLIE

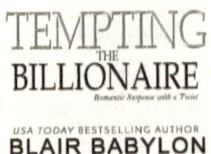

TEMPTING
THE
BILLIONAIRE
Romantic Suspense with a Twist

USA TODAY BESTSELLING AUTHOR
BLAIR BABYLON

Kylie silently freaked out.

Her hands cramped around the arms of the chair, her fingernails digging into the soft leather.

Clawing her way through the wall of the plane wouldn't work and was probably a bad idea, especially now that the airplane had left behind the land mass of North America and was flying over the silver-streaked wavelets of the Atlantic Ocean.

She was an idiot, a dumbass idiot Benny, for getting on an airplane to a foreign country with a fake ID.

But sprinting away from Micah *without her damned phone* because he still had it, with nothing on her person except some maxed-out credit cards and too few stacks of C-notes from Salvatore Grande's office had seemed worse.

Her stupid survival plan was to make her way to the US Embassy in London, assuming that's where the plane really was headed, and throw herself on their mercy.

The embassy *had* to believe Kylie was an American.

With an accent like hers, she couldn't be from *anywhere* but New Jersey.

But she would have to tell the embassy her real name.

She just hoped Chiarina Merlino wasn't on a terrorist watch list or something. Considering her mobbed-up father, her whole family might be on Homeland Security's no-fly list. She might walk into the US Embassy looking for help and perp-walk out in handcuffs.

And if the G-men took her into custody, Salvatore Grande would assume she was squealing. He would hunt down Kylie's mother and sister and kill them just for the optics.

This was so bad.

What Kylie really needed was her goddamn phone. If she had her phone, she could call the embassy to suss out the temperature and decide whether to go there or at least call her friends to help her.

Her social media and bank accounts were set up with two-factor authentication leading *to her phone.* She hadn't memorized any of her thirteen-digit passwords that looked like they were written in Alpha Centauri alien language or even her friends' phone numbers. Who even memorized phone numbers these days? Remembering people's social media handles was more practical.

Kylie needed her *phone,* and she needed to hang onto it.

Micah had shoved it in the backpack with the paintings he'd stolen when he'd plucked it out of her hand that morning, but he'd fidgeted with that bag every chance he'd gotten. He might have moved it.

Indeed, he *probably* had.

She should frisk Micah Shine and see if her phone was on him and, if it wasn't, riffle through his goddamn luggage.

Somehow, she needed to get her hands on him and his bags.

Micah was sitting across the table from her, drinking champagne. She'd been playing footsie with him to keep him riled up and distracted, a technique that procured diamond earrings for her on more occasions than it should have. Men were just so *men* sometimes. Served them right.

Kylie's head became lighter for a moment, a floating sensation like cresting over a hill in a car.

Over the intercom, the pilot said, "We've reached cruising altitude. Please feel free to move about the cabin if you weren't already."

Micah lowered his chin, and his glittering teal gaze turned predatory.

A thrill ran over her ribs and trailed down her belly.

Damn, he did that well.

Nervousness followed the frisson. *Phone.* Her mission was her *phone.*

Kylie stood and raised an eyebrow at him before she turned and sashayed toward the back of the plane.

Air bumped the plane, and the floor swayed under her feet. Kylie gripped the chair as she walked toward the tail-end.

The pocket door to the bathroom was cracked open, and the interior was dark.

Inside the galley, Fothergill the butler was shoving something in a tiny door in the steel cabinets. A whiff of broiling meat drifted through the dry air. His studious ignorance of her standing there seemed to be on purpose.

Yeah, people probably screwed on private jets all the time. He'd probably seen many giggly women entering tiny bathrooms with determined men, or any other permutation of humanity, too.

Kylie hadn't taken her impending walk of shame back down the airplane's center aisle into consideration. Maybe they shouldn't—

Above her head, Micah's big hand pressed against the door, and his gruff voice growled, *"Inside."*

Kylie was swept into the bathroom like a hurricane gust had blown her in.

Inside, the bathroom was a tiny three-quarters model with a glassed-in shower like a bank's pneumatic tube but sized for people. Kylie would probably be fine in there, but Micah had better be careful or he'd end up with bruised elbows.

Maybe shoulders, too.

The door squeaked when it closed. Kylie's shoulders were grabbed, and she was turned so that she was looking in the mirror.

Micah loomed over her head. He growled near her ear. "Pull that flirty little skirt of yours up around your waist."

Kylie's hands shook. They were on a plane thousands of feet above the Atlantic Ocean. What if there was turbulence? Could they even hear a pilot's announcement while in there, asking them to return to their seats because of *something dangerous?* She didn't know what that might be. She'd never been on a plane before. *It all seemed very unnatural.*

What didn't seem unnatural was Micah's fingers sneaking inside the elastic band of her panties around her hips and slowly pushing them down until they dropped to her ankles. He said, "Step out of them."

Kylie lifted one foot and then the other, carefully placing her high-heeled pumps on the vibrating floor and making sure not to spear Micah's foot through his tan dress loafers.

He dragged her panties aside with one foot and glared at her through the mirror. "Unbutton your dress."

Kylie's white dress buttoned all the way from her neck to the hem, so she held her skirt up around her waist with one hand and used her other to push the small buttons through their holes with trembling fingers.

As she finagled the buttons, Micah smoothed his hands over her bare hips, his strong fingers grasping her ass and thighs as they moved on her skin. He wasn't massaging her, although his hands on her felt wonderful. His hands were *possessing* her, stroking her contours as something *his* to toy with.

He bent and ran his lips from the soft spot behind her ear to her neck.

Kylie melted, utterly unable to resist him and past thinking about walks of shame or repercussions.

Or anything else.

She unbuttoned her dress past her bra. The bodice parted.

Micah reached behind her back with one hand and unclasped her bra with a flick.

Yeah, he was way too good at *that,* but Kylie didn't even think about it as her breasts relaxed with their restraint gone.

Micah's lips moved against her shoulder as he whispered, "Keep going."

She unbuttoned her dress to her waist, and Micah slipped his hand under her loose bra to cradle her breast, massaged her as he held her weight in his palm, and ran his thumb over her nipple until it beaded and her whole body was covered with goosebumps.

Kylie leaned against his muscled body behind her, sighing. She was still wearing her high heels, which swayed her back and made her ass press against his jeans. The hard rod of his erection inside his Levi's ground against her.

Micah ran his hands down her arms and pressed her hands against the end of the sink counter. Her skirt fell around her knees. The sharp granite edge of the countertop creased Kylie's palms.

His voice vibrated over her neck as he said, "Don't let go of the counter."

She grasped the edge with her fingertips, trying to obey, but Micah moved his hand away from her breast and flipped her skirt aside, reaching under her dress and between her legs.

His warm fingertip slid over the nub of her clit, already swollen with want, and his other hand came up to work her other breast—grasping, stroking, pinching—in a way that reminded her of his mouth on her.

The intensity of the pleasure from his hands drawing on the peak of her nipple and caressing her clit, slipping inside her softness to find her already wet for him, spun her head like the plane was cresting over the tops of the waves far below the floor beneath her feet. Because her high-heeled shoes bowed her back, his finger dragged against her most sensitive parts as he reached back to find her center, slipped inside, and returned to circle the center of nerves that set fire to her body.

She was squirming and whimpering, rolling her head against his shoulder, when he pushed her from behind and bent her over the countertop.

Foil ripped and latex snapped, and then Micah grabbed a thick fistful of her hair and dragged her head up to look at the mirror above the sink.

In the mirror, he towered over where she was lying with

her dress crumpled around her waist and her bare ass in the air.

His eyes snapped with blazing blue electricity. *"Watch,"* he said, his low voice a command she had to obey. *"Watch while I fuck you."*

He held onto her hair as the pressure against her core became insistent, parting her body as he shoved himself against her and slipped inside. She couldn't drop her head or look away from his gaze, spellbound.

His cock pressed into her body, a deep pressure inside. Once he was in, he reached around her hip and stroked her clit, a hard rub timed with each stroke of him inside her.

Kylie wanted to drop her head, wanted to close her eyes and hide from the intensity of it. As her eyelids drooped, his fingers tightened in her hair, pulling, and he shook her skull. "Open your eyes, little toy. I told you to *watch*."

She stretched her shoulders as he stroked into her, filling her. "What if I don't?"

"I'll cram my cock in your ass and make you watch while I fuck that. Just keep your eyes closed if that's what you want."

Not in an airplane bathroom, not so uncontrolled, for her first time like that.

Kylie fluttered her eyes open and found him staring at her, his opal-blue eyes narrowed with a concentrated lust that looked like rage.

His body rippled as he pulsed into her, his hand drawing the pleasure into a tighter knot between her legs, his attention intent on Kylie's face as she struggled to keep her eyelids open. He took her, squeezed her into a burning star of desire between his hand and his cock, and with a hard rub across her clit as he rammed himself inside—she broke.

Waves of ecstasy twisted her, her legs wobbling as she

rested her weight on the counter and held onto the edge. She rolled, trying to get away from his touch and his cock boring into her oversensitive sex, but he didn't let her escape and forced *another* orgasm to roll through her body, racking her as the world went dark.

Her head was jerked up by her hair. *"Open your eyes."*

Kylie's eyes fluttered, and she watched as he used her body like the little toy she was.

His body spasmed, stabbing up into her, and he pushed deep inside her and held her hips on his cock, groaning as his eyes squeezed shut and creased. For a moment, his release tore away his mask of violence, leaving naked vulnerability.

Inside her, he pulsed, a throb within her raw flesh.

Micah shook his head, gasping, and his expression solidified into stone again. He held onto the condom as he pulled himself out. Knotting it, he tossed it in the trash and then wiped himself off with a towel that he threw in a hole in the cabinet labeled *Hamper*.

Kylie hadn't moved. Her legs vibrated with weakness.

He grabbed her hair again, turning her head to growl into her ear, "Clean yourself up, or I'll use that lubrication running down your legs to take your ass. I won't resist you forever. I *can't*."

After zipping his pants, he left the bathroom and closed the door.

Kylie pried her fingers slowly from the edge of the counter, making sure she wouldn't collapse the second she let go.

Her whole body was sore from the ferocity with which he'd taken her, and the last tremors of the orgasms, *plural,* zinged through her muscles like ricocheting bullets.

Dammit, she'd forgotten to frisk him for her phone.

13

THE ACTORS WHO PLAY WILLIAM AND KATE

MICAH

TEMPTING
THE
BILLIONAIRE
Romantic Suspense with a Twist

USA TODAY BESTSELLING AUTHOR
BLAIR BABYLON

Six and a half hours, five time zones, two sumptuous meals, and one magnum of champagne later, Micah led Kylie off the private jet and into a small terminal at Heathrow that served VIPs of all sorts. One had to know whom to contact to access it, of course.

The city of London they'd flown over had been a starburst of twinkling lights in the vast expanse of the darkness of the Atlantic Ocean. The plane had dived into the heart of the lights until the bright pinpricks resolved into red and yellow lines leading to a terminal at Heathrow Airport.

As they strode in past the deep leather seats and the espresso bar, Micah spied Arthur Finch-Hatten sitting in one of the chairs, reading a book.

He changed course. Kylie stumbled at his quick pivot, but he had an arm around her at her first bobble, holding her up.

Her plush form against his side sent a scattering of desire through his body, and he resisted the urge to smash her up against a wall and kiss the stuffing out of her, turning it into a quick squeeze instead.

They were among the British now.

Propriety must be preserved.

As Micah approached, Arthur glanced up, saw him, and stood in one athletic motion before turning and walking away from Micah and Kylie without a backward glance.

Oh, tradecraft.

Right. Never knew who might be watching.

Micah followed Arthur unobtrusively through the small terminal, veering away from Arthur's wake as he'd been taught, but followed him around a corner and into a small room.

Inside, Arthur closed the door behind them.

Kylie immediately piped up. "Did you see who was out there? Was that Prince William and Princess Kate?"

Arthur told her gently, "It wouldn't have been. The royal family has a suite of their own. You might have noticed actors who play them on television, however."

Micah's Sicilian genes that loved to talk and gossip rose to the forefront. "About the royal family, what you think about—"

The subtle wince between Arthur's eyebrows stopped Micah from blabbing further. "Members of the royal family come and go and change importance with alarming frequency these days. My family's interest has always been a longer-term view of power politics. If we had time, we could discuss how money from outside the UK influences our government and public perception. *That* actually matters. In the meantime, I believe you said you needed *this.*"

Arthur handed Micah a small blue booklet and continued. "We inserted information into the US databases to match the passport, including a government identification number from the US Social Security Administration. It should pass muster at any port of entry or for any other purpose, as it was issued by our cousins in the US. We bashed it up a bit, lest it appear too conspicuously new."

Micah flipped open the stiff cover of the US passport, finding the first page with Kylie's picture that listed the bearer as Kylie Margaret Miller, born in Atlantic City, New Jersey. It was a good picture of her, taken with her hair behind her ears on a white background. "Where'd you get the picture?"

Arthur shrugged. "It's a composite from social media. A little here, a little there, and we have a photo."

Micah handed it to Kylie. "Here you are. You don't ever have to worry about ID again."

Kylie's eyes filled with tears, and she covered her mouth with her hand as she stared at the passport.

She asked, "Why is my middle name *Margaret?*"

14

KYLIE MILLER

KYLIE

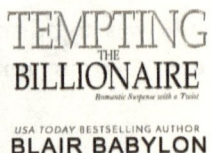

ylie held the passport in her hand.

An official United States passport.

One that could be used for any purpose like procuring a real driver's license, boarding any plane, or getting a job.

With this stupid little booklet holding a picture of herself that she'd never seen before printed inside it, the name *Kylie Miller* became a real person who was a citizen of the United States.

She could be Kylie Miller forever.

She could be safe.

Chiarina Merlino could be officially gone and rest in peace.

Her life was indescribably different.

Her throat closed, and she choked out, "Did you just say that you made me a Social Security Number, *too?*"

"Certainly," the new ridiculously tall guy said. His black hair waved on the sides and was cut neatly but not military-short. But his eyes were what caught Kylie's attention. She would've thought that she would be immune to pretty eyes by now, what with Micah having teal-sparked aqua eyes that glimmered and Logan with his bright emerald eyes.

But this guy, *wow.*

His eyes were pale silver, shining like precious metal, and sharp as a polished steel knife.

"Thank you," Kylie said, her voice breathless. "I mean, I can't thank you enough. *Thank you.*"

The new guy's smile was tight and secretive, and he clasped Micah's shoulder. "Anything for my best boy."

15

KNIGHTSBRIDGE
ARTHUR FINCH-HATTEN

L ord Arthur Finch-Hatten, Earl of Severn, left his two guests with his wife in the kitchen of his Knightsbridge penthouse and retreated to his private study to examine the thumb drives Micah had utilized to hack Salvatore Grande's computer.

When they'd entered the flat, Arthur had ignored his view overlooking Hyde Park outside the floor-to-ceiling windows, but his guests had stopped, stunned. The building was located in Knightsbridge, one of the poshest parts of London, halfway between Kensington Palace and Buckingham Palace.

The woman who was with Micah, now legally named Kylie Miller, had exclaimed, "What is it with your friends and windows looking at the tops of trees?"

Micah chuckled.

Kylie rounded on Arthur. "So, is this another eight-million-dollar view?"

Arthur had raised one eyebrow at her, bemused. American frankness was jarring but entertaining. "I'm sure I wouldn't know the price."

Arthur's lovely wife, the Lady Genevieve Finch-Hatten, Countess of Severn, had taken Micah and Kylie under her wing and shooed them into the kitchen for a late-night snack even though they protested they'd been fed to their gills on the plane. Gen's Texas hospitality would not take no for an answer, though, and he'd left the three of them snacking on fruit and cheese.

Arthur had chuckled to himself about Kylie's "tops of trees" remark as he walked away, knowing they'd stayed across the street from Central Park in New York City the previous night. Arthur's tracking application on Micah's phone had tattled, a little piece of code that Arthur had installed the last time Micah had so readily logged onto the Wi-Fi at Arthur's country estate when he'd visited to "walk in the deer park." The covert app wasn't malicious, though it was without Micah's permission. Arthur kept tabs on his agents as they ran around the world, collecting information and doing his bidding. He'd saved several of their lives and ferreted out double agents that way, so it was for the best for everyone.

The thumb drives Micah had used to clone Salvatore Grande's computer had been Arthur's own devices.

Supposedly, Kylie Miller had a mother and sister somewhere in the world, Sofia and Rachele Merlino, respectively, and Grande had threatened them as if he'd known where they were. Their location was one question of many Micah had securely emailed Arthur earlier in the day.

Arthur stripped the protective layers of code from the mirror image of the Mafia don's hard drive.

Within minutes, he'd decrypted the data.

He sat back in his chair, staring at just how far down the proverbial rabbit hole of the criminal underworld Micah had fallen.

This was bad.
Very bad.

16

IT'S ALWAYS MONACO

KYLIE

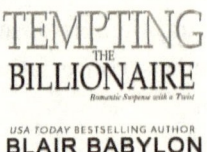

Okay, Her Majesty the Honorable Countess Gen Finch-Hatten was fabulicious.

It was eleven o'clock at night in London but only suppertime back home in Atlantic City. She'd napped on the plane after getting plowed in the bathroom, and Kylie was *wired* and ready to talk.

Luckily, Gen was ready to talk back.

They talked, laughed, and destroyed the cheese and fruit platter on the stainless steel kitchen island. Micah had loosened up to the point where he was leaning on his elbows while he popped grapes in his mouth between laughs. He was still talking with that brisk British accent of his, which finally seemed appropriate now that they were in London.

Gen badgered Kylie into telling her whole story about how Kylie had met Micah.

"And then this wiseguy shows up in my section when I was waitressing *again*." Kylie backhanded Micah, who chuckled and ate another sphere of mozzarella from the board between them. "And I, like some ditz, was like, 'Surely nothing bad will happen to me if I trust him *again*.'"

Gen laughed with a loud Texas chortle. "What could go wrong?"

"*Right?* And so, everything got more complicated from there."

"As it does."

"*Yeah,* it did."

Kylie was just about to spill it all when Arthur strolled into the kitchen, his hands in his trouser pockets and a grave expression that stopped the conversation dead.

"Arthur?" Gen asked.

Micah straightened. "What did you find?"

"Enough," Arthur said.

"Did you find my sister?" Kylie asked him, hoping and almost hoping not, wishing Rachele was somewhere untraceably safe. "Is my mom with her?"

Arthur pressed his lips together and looked down at his shoes, hesitating before he said, "I think they are together."

"Where?" Kylie rounded the kitchen island and strode over to him. When a terrifying thought assailed her, she almost stumbled but held herself upright because the women in her family didn't fall apart in front of others. "*Are they alive?*"

Arthur nodded but didn't look up. "As far as I can ascertain, they both appear to be alive."

"And together?"

"And together," he agreed.

Relief flooded Kylie, tinged with the loneliness and jealousy of those left behind. "And they're okay?"

"That, I don't know," Arthur said.

"I'm tired of this twenty-questions guessing game," Kylie said. "Just goddamn tell me already. Should we come to look at your computer or something?"

Both Arthur and Gen said, "No," in unison.

Interesting. "Then what is it?"

Arthur had grabbed an orange section from the mostly depopulated snack board and was chewing it.

They waited.

He swallowed. "A few years ago—"

"Oh my God," Kylie said, flopping forward like a dropped marionette. "I can't handle this. Tell me the name of the country or state they're in or *something.*"

Arthur said, "Monaco."

Micah rolled his eyes. "Of course, it's Monaco. It's always goddamn Monaco. How does so much mayhem happen in that postage stamp of a country that isn't long enough for a proper jog?"

Arthur raised one dark eyebrow at Micah.

Micah's eyes drifted up in what looked like a repressed eyeroll. "Yes. Quite."

Kylie had heard enough of this yammering. "This is my *sister* and my *mom* we're talking about. *Will you goddamn make sense?*"

Arthur nodded. "I apologize. Of course, but there's a lot to it. How much do you know about the Russian mafia?"

"*Russian* mafia?" Kylie repeated and thought herself stupid. "Russians bratvas aren't *Mafia.* Russian crime organizations *aren't* La Cosa Nostra, *this thing of ours.* A lot of LCN syndicates specify you have to be half Sicilian to be *made.* Not the Camorra, of course. They're from Napoli. For them, it's just half-*Italian.* If they're *Russians,* they aren't *Mafia.* They aren't *family.* I mean, I know bratvas exist. I know they do things like drugs, prostitution, and human trafficking that, traditionally, Italian families wouldn't *touch.* The Italian organizations do business with the Russians when necessary, not that I know anything about the Russian bratvas or the Italian Mafia or anything like that."

No, *that* sounded stupid.

She added, "I mean, I didn't finish high school. I was studying to get my GED. I really don't know anything about anything. Especially the Mafia."

Arthur finished chewing a chunk of something white-fleshed with black seeds and looked up at her with his silver eyes. "You don't have to pretend with us, Kylie. My ancestors are pillaging marauders and genocidal murderers back to the Norman Conquest, which is how I inherited unfathomable wealth."

Gen, standing beside her husband, rolled her eyes. "He actually inherited a crumbling earldom, which, with one wrong move, would have gone bankrupt and vanished. He did a hell of a job rebuilding it. Ask him about the bricks on his manor house sometime."

Arthur patted her hand and smiled softly. "But my point, Kylie, is that you are who *you* are, and having certain knowledge gleaned from one's family isn't a crime."

Micah was watching her, too.

Kylie examined a fat red grape, mottled with green, that she held in her fingertips. Behind it, the three adults staring at her were blurred to smears of color. "I know *some stuff* about Salvatore Grande's Philly operation. I know that he murdered my father for being a rat, even though my father *wasn't* a rat. Somebody fingered him when he hadn't done anything wrong, maybe so they could move up in Grande's organization. But I don't want to know anything else. I want to leave Philly and never go back. But whatever I do, I *have to know* where my mother and Rachele are."

She refocused her eyes past the grape.

The rest of the kitchen and Arthur sharpened into view. He said, "So you don't know anything about *Russian* organized crime."

"My father wouldn't have done business with the Russian bratvas. He was *traditional.*"

Arthur nodded slowly. "A Russian bratva colloquially known as the *Chekhovskaya bratva* operates in that region. Your mother and sister have been seen in the presence of men who are associated with the *Chekhovskaya* bratva and traveling in cars registered to people known to be associated."

"So, they're just hanging out in Europe?" Kylie asked, her heart falling apart.

"It seems that your sister and mother are in some way associated with the *Chekhovskaya* bratva, or in the same location as them." He paused. "Or they've been detained by them."

Shock popped through Kylie. *"Detained? Like, kidnapped?"*

Micah, meanwhile, sighed more heavily. "The *Chekhovskaya?* They're powerful. They took over much of that region when the Sokolovs had those *setbacks* last year."

Arthur nodded as he answered Micah. "Bratvas are notoriously nimble. When an operation loses influence, a few months of chaos results until power consolidates in another organization. The bratvas recruit members based on talent and vileness rather than by nationality, which is why they're expanding so rapidly. They control most of the former Soviet bloc states utterly. Their syndicates are wiping out Italian Mafias all over the world. The Italian Mafia will cease to exist within twenty years, probably ten. They might not be entirely wiped out in Sicily, *maybe.* Or a bratva may want to make a statement and do it."

Kylie leaned in. *"Hey,* duke of *earl.* My *mom* and my *sister.* Kidnapped or *not?"*

Arthur shook his head. "I don't know. The language is

unclear as to whether they're being held as guests, assets, hostages, or prisoners."

"But they're *being held?*" she asked for clarification.

"There seems to be some talk of restraint or limitations," he admitted.

"You found this info on Grande's computer?"

Arthur Finch-Hatten nodded, still grim.

Steel-cold rage iced her veins. "Is Salvatore *fucking* Grande involved? Did he set these *Chekhovskaya* up to *kidnap my family?*"

"That's possible. Initial communications between Grande and the Russians began about a month before the date they went missing. That's the right time frame. The communications have continued since." Arthur glanced at Micah for some reason. Micah was staring at the cheese-board remnants on the kitchen island, so Arthur looked back at Kylie. "But the communications have continued. It appears to be an ongoing relationship."

Images of her mother or sister lying cold and dirty in a Russian basement assailed Kylie. She'd been mad because they'd left without her or that Grande had relocated them and not her.

Maybe Kylie had been terribly, horribly *wrong.*

But they'd taken *clothes.* And a *suitcase.* And her mom's *purse* and their *passports.*

It wasn't clear-cut.

Kylie covered her face and sank to her elbows on the kitchen island. "Oh my God."

Feminine hands patted her and wrapped around her shoulders. Gen said, "I'm so sorry. We'll do everything we can to get more information. *Won't we?*"

That last part seemed to be addressed to the other side of the island.

Micah asked, "Their kidnapping couldn't have been in retribution *for* anything, could it?"

Kylie dragged her hands down her face to see Arthur and Micah exchanging volumes of conversation without a word.

Arthur shook his head, an efficient gesture with no subterfuge in it. "Time frames don't match in the slightest. Kylie's mother and sister disappeared *four years* ago. Your prior scuffle with the Sokolovs on Maxence's behalf was less than a year ago, and you *met* Kylie only recently. Nothing adds up. It's not *you*."

Kylie said, "It was retribution for my father being a rat, or rather because they *thought* he was a rat, but he wasn't. That's what it had to be. His murder was a message job through the mouth. Grande's been exploiting me for years in revenge for it and threatened worse. Are you *sure* they're still alive?" she asked Arthur.

"That's the odd part," Arthur said. "The communications, even recent ones, refer to both of them in the present tense. 'They *are*. She *is*.' They're likely both alive and in or near Monaco."

"Because?"

"Monaco and the surrounding areas of France are the *Chekhovskaya* base of operations now. They described a certain warehouse district as a possible location for them."

A warehouse. *Jesus, Mary, and Joseph.*

Micah asked Arthur, "Can't we just get Maxence to pick up the country and shake it and see if they fall out? You're his friend, and he owes me."

"This is more than Maxence can do," Arthur told him and included Kylie in the conversation with a glance. "It's too soon. There's been too much chaos. Maxence's position is far from secure. He was *just* enthroned as the Sovereign Prince of Monaco."

"I beg your pardon?" Kylie asked. "This guy is *what?*"

"It's the boarding school I went to for high school, again," Micah said. "Maxence was the younger brother of the heir to the throne of Monaco, but he ended up with it. Half the royalty and billionaires in the world sent their kids to Le Rosey to get them out of their hair and keep them safe from whatever was after them."

"So, how did *you* get into that school?" Kylie asked him.

Micah shrugged. "Scholarship."

For just a fraction of a second, Arthur's glance at Micah hardened, and his eyes narrowed. The look on his face smoothed to neutrality almost before Kylie recognized what was there. If Arthur hadn't been standing so close to Micah, she wouldn't have caught the change out of the corner of her eye.

That wasn't a sudden quiver of realization. Arthur *knew* something about Micah and didn't like whatever it was.

But Micah had seen it, too. "If Max can't help, I know my way around Monaco. We can stay with Twist on his boat while we ask around."

Arthur's reply was so light that Kylie was instantly suspicious. "Are you sure that's wise?"

"Absolutely," Micah said.

Kylie asked Micah, "So, how soon can we use this shiny new passport of mine and get to Monaco?"

"As soon as we have a plan in place," Arthur said. "A few days at most. It takes a bit to refuel and maintain the jet."

"Okay, I should probably sleep," Kylie said. "If we're going rescuin' tomorrow."

"I'll show you to a guest room," Gen said, steering her out of the kitchen.

When they were in the hall, Kylie asked, "What was going on between those two?"

Gen Finch-Hatten shook her head, her lips pressed in a hard line. "I don't know. There's something, though. But Arthur can't tell me everything, even if he wanted to, and I couldn't pass it on if I wanted to." She looked back at Kylie. "It's part of his *job.*"

Oh.

And that made Micah . . . *what, exactly?*

17

MARCU

MICAH

TEMPTING
THE
BILLIONAIRE
Romantic Suspense with a Twist

USA TODAY BESTSELLING AUTHOR
BLAIR BABYLON

The women left the kitchen.

Micah stuffed another ball of muzz into his mouth, and the buffalo-milk mozzarella embraced his molars like an Italian nonna's hug. Knowing Arthur's refined tastes, it was probably straight from Naples. And yet knowing Arthur's bent toward personal responsibility and climate change, Micah bet Arthur had bought it for his wife.

Arthur turned back to Micah, looking him straight in the eyes. "What the fuck are you doing?"

Micah scowled at him. "What the fuck am I doing with *what?*"

"The Sokolovs have a price on your head and your codswallop friends, and they are based in Monaco. They haven't taken you out because their organization was in disarray after Matryona Sokolov went to prison and Kir was killed. Their priorities were restructuring rather than chasing you around Europe and the States. But they did restructure. They've made inroads in the US and Europe, although the *Chekhovskaya* swept in and took over Monaco and its environs. Are you trying to remind them that you exist?"

Micah shrugged. "They probably don't even remember me."

Arthur shook his head. "Believing that will get you both killed."

"Kylie's sister and her mother are all she has left. She won't stop looking for them."

"You call her Kylie instead of Chiarina, do you?"

"Her name is Kylie now. She has an official US passport to prove it. If her family is still alive, we have to see this through. She's not going to be able to live with herself if we don't."

"And you don't think *your* family's murders have anything to do with your decision?"

"What the hell do you know about that?" Micah demanded, and his New York accent thickened in his mouth. "You don't have the right to go poking your nose into what happened to them."

Arthur's eyes narrowed. "Do you think I would recruit you without knowing *exactly* who you were?"

"You've known all this time?" Micah grated out.

"It's never been important before. I recruited you because you're good at what you do, and what *you* do is the job description of what *I* do. All the best spies are con artists."

Micah stepped toward Arthur, panic and rage twisting his fingers into fists. *"I'm not a con artist.* I've been straight for *years.* Shine Industries is a well-reputed organization that has never done a shady deal. I haven't had to *talk* anyone into *anything* in years because it's a solid business."

Arthur didn't flinch. His disinterested smile didn't even jitter. "Keep your voice down, *Marcu.* Kylie will hear you.

And you are one of the most *persuasive* men I've ever met, with the possible exception of His Serene Highness Maxence of Monaco. Max brings people around with his preternatural charisma, though. You *talk* people into doing what you want." Arthur's cold smile didn't reach his eyes. "Which is exactly why you're my best boy."

Ah, the British, with their subtle references to the British version of a school class president at upper-class boarding schools that set you exactly in your place, which was as their lackey, but a good one. Prized above all others, as a matter of fact.

Arthur tilted his head to the side. "Tell me, exactly when did this operation turn from hitting back at the organized crime syndicates trying to tear down civilization to you becoming an errand boy for that girl in my guest bedroom?"

And the British certainly knew how to sucker punch but turn it into a question to make it seem so pleasant. "It's not."

Arthur turned and gestured with an orange section. "Of course. Let's have a scotch and discuss how you're going to enter Monaco without getting yourself and that pretty little girl horribly murdered for your trouble, and what you're going to do for *me* in the process."

18

BADA-BING, BADA-BOOM

KYLIE

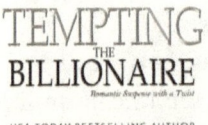

"**S**o, we're *not* rescuing them? You want to pull some kind of a con instead?" Kylie asked Micah.

No flippin' way.

She had not come all the way to London, *almost* all the way to Europe, to run a con that meant she would leave *without even looking for her mom and Rachele.*

Was that what Micah and Arthur had been planning?

Because *no way.*

Kylie had been hanging out in the London penthouse with Gen all morning while Arthur and Micah had been *planning.* Gen was from Texas and had the twang to prove it, but somehow, she was a British lawyer, like one who went to court wearing a wig and robe and made speeches defending people. Gen was *interesting,* and Kylie kind of wanted to be her when she grew up. Not a lawyer, exactly. But *something.*

Kylie wanted to be *something.*

She'd never met someone who was *something* before or something that she wanted to *be.* Lots of people she'd met were something Kylie didn't want to end up as.

Micah and Arthur Finch-Hatten had been hiding in a

home office at the back of the central London penthouse all morning, presumably talking about the plan to get Kylie's mother and sister back.

Now Kylie and Micah were back in the guest bedroom with the king-size bed and an expensive view overlooking the treetops of Hyde Park, the one with an enormous, tufted chaise lounge that seemed to be the size of a California twin bed in the sitting area.

Kylie was clacking her proverbial steak tongs because she was planning to *grill* Micah until he told her *everything* he and Arthur Finch-Hatten had supposedly concocted.

But that didn't mean *she* was going along with it.

"We're rescuing them," Micah said. "Or we're doing whatever needs to be done to get them out of Europe and away from the bratva or whoever has them, by whatever name you want to call it."

Kylie squinted at him. "That *sounds* like we're rescuing them, and it had better mean that because I'm not doing anything else *until* we rescue them."

"Yes," Micah said. "We're rescuing them."

"Did you find out where they are?"

"Not exactly."

"Then we don't exactly have a plan."

"We've found some discussion of your sister being at a warehouse in France just outside of Monaco, but your mother's whereabouts are more—"

"Unknown?"

"Elusive."

"But she's alive."

"We have no indication that she's not."

"Is all of this from Salvatore Grande's computer?"

Micah shook his head. "Arthur has other sources."

"He's a spy."

"I wouldn't say that."

"So he's not a spy?"

"He has connections."

"Does he have the kind of connections that can rescue my mother and sister?"

"No."

"Because they need rescuing," Kylie told him, even though an odd vibration in her lower belly made her feel sick. "They wouldn't have left without me unless they were forced to. I mean, I was *sixteen*. My mom wouldn't have ditched me when I was *sixteen* unless she'd been forced to, right?"

"Of course not," Micah said, and it seemed like he'd jumped on that too quickly. "No one would have. She must have thought she was saving you."

"I mean, we were fighting a lot. Because I was sixteen."

Micah nodded. "Fighting between parents and teenagers is probably common."

"Didn't you fight with your parents?" she asked him.

"I was away at boarding school."

"But not all the time."

"Year-round," he said while hunting through his suitcase, poking his fingers in the bag's side pockets.

"Wow, you didn't even go home for summer or Christmas breaks?"

Micah shrugged as he poked. "Not really. And besides, even if you two were arguing as teenagers argue, she *must* have thought she was saving you when she left. Otherwise, she wouldn't have gone."

The trembling fear in Kylie's stomach belched up her throat, burning, though Kylie just looked out over the treetops of Hyde Park outside the wide window and said without expression, "Or maybe I was just a bad kid."

Micah stood up and stepped over to take her in his arms. "No one would leave their kid, *especially you*, unless they had to. And you *couldn't* have been a bad kid, Kylie. You're funny and sharp, but you aren't an asshole. You had to have been one of the top performers in your little swindling group in Atlantic City. You were giving away money to the other girls every night. That's not a dick move."

"But there were nights when I came up empty, but I still took money home because we all shared the take. It's insurance."

Micah shook his head. "I saw. You and the Hispanic woman—"

"Rita Torres."

"Yeah, her. You two were *always* the top earners."

"But Alma has a baby, and Priyanka was our lookout and accomplice in the jewelry store. She was worth more as an accomplice." Kylie looked up at him. "How long did you watch me before you made your move?"

"Long enough." He smiled down at her. "I'm just saying that you are a kind soul, whether you want to believe it or not. Unless your mother was a psychopath, she left you behind to *save* you, not to abandon you, and she must have known you'd be all right. She trusted you to be all right."

Two jarring notes came together in Kylie's head like a clang, and she leaned back to see Micah's face better. *"What do you want?"*

"I beg your—" His eyes narrowed as he looked down at her. "I don't *want* anything from you."

"I can smell bullshit at a hundred yards, Micah Shine. *This?"* She flipped her finger up and down, indicating their embrace. *"This* is a con job. This kind of reassurance and buttering-up is *exactly* what I do every night in AC to make drunk men think they want to buy me jewelry or give me gambling money that I pocket. If there's one thing you've taught me, it's to recognize when *I'm the mark.*"

He untangled his arms from her and stepped back. "You're not the mark."

"Then *who is?*"

"It depends on how you look at it. We're going into a dangerous situation to rescue your mother and your sister, and I have no reason to go. There's no upside for me in this at all. So if there's a mark, *I'm* the mark."

She kept watching him, trying to see the tattletale twitches that would tell her what he was thinking. "But there's a plan."

"Yeah, the plan is to go into Monaco and let it be known—"

"That sounds squishy," she said.

"I know a guy, okay?" Micah asked her. "We'll *let it be known* that we have a rare and valuable painting for sale to a *discreet* bidder."

The backpack containing the two aforementioned rare and valuable paintings *and presumably her damned phone* had been handed to Arthur Finch-Hatten and hidden away the night before.

"That's not going to work," she said. "We're going to draw all kinds of criminals out of the woodwork with the scent of black-market art, not just the ones who kidnap innocent mothers and sisters in Philadelphia."

"But we know who to look for, meaning we're looking for someone associated with the *Chekhovskaya bratva*. We'll use *them* to get to whoever is running Monaco these days."

Kylie fretted, "This sounds *very* squishy. And what worries me is that when you double-cross a Russian bratva, they kill you."

"But we'll be long gone."

"But they have long reach," she reminded him.

"But I have friends who will *block* that reach," he told her.

Kylie asked him, *"Who?"*

"What do you mean, who?"

"Who? *Who* could influence a Russian bratva to leave us alone if we cheat them?"

"But we're not going to *cheat* them. We're going to look at their operation and their warehouse or other places you could hide two people for four years. We will find your sister and your mother and then rescue them."

"This is confusing," Kylie said.

"No, it's not confusing," Micah said as he went back to poking through his luggage. "We're using the paintings as bait. Criminals like bait, or at least they like stolen paintings. Some of those criminals will be *Chekhovskaya* because we'll be in Monaco, and Monaco is where the *Chekhovskaya* are. Once we find them, *bada-bing, bada-boom,* we find your sister and your mother."

"Did you just *bada-bing* me?" Kylie demanded. "Did you, *rice cake,* did you just *bada-bing me?"*

He spread his arms. "I'm just sayin' that it's all going to go according to plan, and if anyone's the mark, *I'm* the mark. Now, you need to go with Gen to buy you a dress for the ball because we'll let it be known that we have black market art to sell at a charity event in Monaco. And for that, I need a tux, and you need a dress."

"You're never the mark," Kylie muttered as she stomped out of the room to go with Gen to buy a ball gown.

19

TRISTAN KING
MICAH

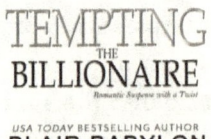

USA TODAY BESTSELLING AUTHOR
BLAIR BABYLON

Micah hadn't seen Tristan "Twist" King for several months.

The Scholarship Mafia group chat that the four of them used was active as hell, so Micah knew where Twist was in the world and how his breakfast had been digested, but they hadn't seen each other for a while.

Micah and Kylie strolled up the wooden sidewalk floating on pontoons to the rear of Twist's yacht, a vessel that could have been appropriately called an ocean-going ship, docked in a superyacht row of the Monaco Yacht Club in Port Hercule, Principality of Monaco.

Sea water lapped the cement quays and floating docks between the boats, and the eternal swirling scourge of seagulls cawed and stole anything remotely edible from careless people, dogs, and stray cats.

Micah carried the specially constructed case holding the paintings they'd stolen from Salvatore Grande. His palm began to sweat on the sun-warmed handle at the thought of dropping the case and it slipping into the sea below the floating sidewalk, cresting, flipping, and sinking the salt water-destroyed art. The idea nauseated him so much that his feet felt the movement under the platform even more.

A porter from the yacht club ferried their two suitcases behind them, and Micah called out, *"Ahoy!* Isn't that what you're supposed to yell, Twist? Are you here?"

The Mediterranean sun was bright over the azure sea, and cool air trickled down his shirt collar. Late fall in temperate Monaco was pleasant compared to the wintry chill of the US East Coast and foggy London. The Monegasques probably considered the sunny weather chilly for late-October, but it was a gorgeous day for Micah's native New Yorker bones.

Twist's superyacht was a three-story behemoth that didn't quite qualify for megayacht status, which is why it could dock inside the marina of the Monaco Yacht Club. Twist could step off his ship onto the cement quays and walk to the yacht club building and the street beyond. Larger megayachts moored offshore, and their passengers had to be ferried by small motorboat tenders to dry land.

Twist strolled out of his office on the ship's surface-level deck as they approached, and he waved to Micah and Kylie over the Plexiglas railing. "Yeah, hi. Where've you been?"

Beside Micah, Kylie waved. "Hi!"

Twist strolled toward the blunt stern end of his boat, picking his way between the coiled ropes and life vest bins. "And who's this?"

Twist knew exactly who Kylie was from the pics Micah had posted in their group chat with his cover story about what had happened these last few days. He'd posted plausible lies, anticipating subpoenas.

Micah introduced Kylie and Twist while the porter rolled their luggage aboard.

Twist's pallor worried Micah. Twist lived on a *yacht* in

the *Mediterranean Sea,* essentially on the French Riviera. If Monaco was too cold for Twist to soak up some sun, he could sail his boat to Italy's Amalfi Coast or Marrakesh, where the sea and air were ten to twenty degrees warmer. No one who lived there should be so pale.

After greetings in which Micah could not refrain from a possessive hand on the small of Kylie's back even though he'd planned not to make such a move, Kylie trotted off to explore the yacht while Micah talked with Twist.

As she pattered off to the sun decks two stories above the sea, the salt breeze whipped at the trousers she and Gen had gone shopping for in London, molding them against her shapely legs. She drew her jacket more firmly around her waist. The sun cast a golden halo over Kylie's raven curls and golden skin, showering her like it was welcoming her Sicilian blood home.

A slap bonked Micah's arm hard enough to knock him sideways. "What the hell?"

Twist chided him, "Give your suitcase to Jian. He'll take it down to your cabin for you. Stop making googly eyes at the girl and come into my office. I found something."

"I was not making proverbial *googly eyes,*" Micah muttered and followed Twist into the darkness of his office, though he watched Twist's head of staff, Jian, as he made off with the bag containing the priceless works of art.

Blazing computer monitors tiled the back wall of the small office in a tall grid.

Ah, yes, Twist had tipped over the edge from computer scientist to Evil Genius Mastermind.

Micah asked, "Why don't you just use a VR headset?"

"Those things hurt my nose," Twist griped. "I'm not going to end up with some weirdly bent nose when I can cable up an array instead."

"Fair enough. What did you find?"

Twist squinted at him. "Have you been in the UK or hanging out with someone from there?"

"I beg your pardon?" Micah asked.

"Yeah, just like that. You usually have a neutral American accent to cover up your New York accent, but you've gone all the way to the King's English. You sound like Master Hamilton at Le Rosey."

"I do not."

Twist laughed at him. "Sure, you don't."

"It doesn't matter what I sound like this week. What did you find?"

Twist sat in the center of a wide U-desk that occupied most of the room. "Hacking surveillance feeds is always interesting. I assume you took a look with facial recognition to track your targets, too?"

Micah shrugged one shoulder, noncommittal, nonliable. What he had access to or didn't was none of Twist's business, and in some cases, such knowledge might be considered a national security secret to some countries.

"The age-progressed photos of Rachele and Sofia you sent over were helpful," Twist began, firing up sightings of them from the internet. "As you can see here, here, and here," he pointed at still shots in crowds, "they're together at least some of the time, and they move around with at least some degree of freedom."

Most of the surveillance photos were monochrome, or the color was grainy, so Micah leaned in to see better. "You're sure that's them?"

"Not in the slightest. Even the best age-progression software isn't accurate for the puberty years. In the last pictures, Rachele was ten years old, and now she's fourteen. We have an educated guess that's probably wrong."

The pictures of age-progressed Rachele showed a young teenager with medium brown curls and hazel eyes with the chubby cheeks of youth.

Micah asked, "And that's who we're looking for?"

"Yep, which means at least some of these hits are bound to be false positives, if not most of them. If she's in America eating the Standard American Diet of deep-fried white flour soaked in sugar, add twenty pounds. If she picked up ballet, modeling, or smoking at twelve, subtract the same or more. The mother, Sofia, would have been more accurate if we'd had better pictures." Twist flapped his hand at a screen on the top row, left side. "That match puts the Sofia composite in Geneva, and you can see that the woman is wearing big sunglasses and a scarf over her ears. She's even turning away and a little blurred. If this Sofia woman is a prisoner of the Sokolov bratva, we can rule that one out, the ones from Vienna and these others."

He tapped a key, and half the pictures spread over the wall darkened.

"Which leaves us with these, most of which were taken at night in France outside Monaco." The cursor zoomed over the computer monitors, circling over women in crowds who appeared to match the Sofia or Rachele profile as Micah watched. "In these pictures that bear similarity to the age-progressed composites of Rachele and Sofia—"

Which was a whole lot of verbiage meant to cover Twist's ass when this information was wrong.

"—we often see several large men accompanying them, looking both at the women and at others around them. They're obviously armed. They might be guarding them, keeping them from escaping, or both."

One picture showed one of those large men grabbing

the arm of a girl purported to be Rachele, and horror creased the girl's face.

Kylie would climb through the monitor to rescue Rachele if she saw that.

Twist asked him, "Do you think we should get Kylie up here to identify her sister and mother?"

Micah shook his head. "The AI can do a better job of matching at this point than someone who hasn't seen them in over four years, and Kylie doesn't need to know our methods."

Twist frowned, troubled. "If you say so."

"Do we have precise location on these data points?" Micah asked him.

"Down to eight decimal places of latitude and longitude. When I triangulated them and accounted for the roads here, they all came back to this region," Twist said, pointing to a screen showing a satellite image of a grouping of white rectangular buildings surrounded by green circles of bushes or trees. "It's the warehouse district in France, including that warehouse we raided a few months ago, the one rented by the so-called Red Flag Financial Group."

"We should have just swept every warehouse in a two-mile radius for other prisoners."

"There are hundreds," Twist said. "France supplies Monaco with everything except billionaires. Also, if I put these pictures in chronological order, you can see the problem."

With a flip of his wrist, the pictures reassorted themselves on the computer screens.

Micah leaned over the desk, trying to figure out what it meant.

Twist told him, "From the chronological view, we can see that they've been transported or trafficked or relocated regularly. Last year around the time we were busy raiding that warehouse, the Rachele and Sofia targets were in Poland."

Micah gestured to the map at the top of the screens. "Why would the Russian bratva be dragging them all over Europe?"

Twist paused before he answered, "There are a lot of reasons why Russian organized crime syndicates would transport women around Europe, especially a pretty woman like Sofia, who is probably not yet forty years old, or very young ones like Rachele."

Micah needed to keep that information as far away from Kylie as he could. The pain it would inflict on her would enrage him, and he needed to keep his head in the game. "Right. Next step?"

Twist shrugged. "Find out which damn warehouse the *Chekhovskaya* bratva is keeping them in."

"Yeah," Micah said, his eyebrows cramping from frowning. "Easy peasy."

20

PHONE

KYLIE

The stolen paintings had traveled with Kylie and Micah to Monaco, which meant the bag they were in was nearby, too.

And so was Kylie's phone.

Probably.

Micah had told Kylie to expect staff to be on the yacht, yet another thing that blew her mind. Sure, she could see Atlantic City bellhops porting people's bags and hotel maids cleaning their rooms because that was the hotel business, but having a guy who hung around all the time to take care of your stuff for you seemed excessive.

And lazy.

Going on vacation was fun, but living with other people poking into your stuff all the time seemed creepy.

And it wasn't just "a guy" that Twist had working for him, Kylie saw as she explored the *yacht,* the one in *Monaco,* just down the street from a mall dubbed the *"Billionaires' Shopping Center."*

Other people were employed on the ship, too, to wash down the sides of the yacht, shine the clear plastic railing around every deck, bring groceries aboard, and talk to each other and point at things from the conning tower on the very top of the ship. When she'd peeked inside the room on the top deck, screens rising from wide touchscreen controls looked more like a starship command bridge than a boat's wheelhouse. Big radar dishes and globes sprouted from the lookout like the ship might also be used for hunting UFOs.

At least ten people seemed to be employed on the ship, excluding the delivery people.

How could anyone call living like that a *home?* It must be like staying in a hotel all the time.

Twenty minutes of traipsing around the boat later, Kylie found the guest stateroom they'd been assigned to, for their clothes were hanging in the closet and pressed.

Pressed.

The cabin was decorated in stereotypical nautical blue, white, brass trim, and medium wood. The effect was elegant, as if the superyacht would be precisely what it was expected to be, just like any other servant in a livery uniform.

The boxy suitcase containing the stolen paintings leaned in a corner.

Kylie descended on it in a storm of rage, ready to rip the goddamn black nylon to shreds in her quest to find her phone.

But it was in the first outside pocket she looked in.

She pressed her thumbnail to the power button.

The screen lit, and it told her *Hello* and *60%.*

Messages scrolled up the face as she unlocked it.

So many messages were from Rita, Alma, and Priyanka.

She didn't bother to read them but just started typing back, *I'm okay. I'm fine. I'm with the guy, and everything is going fine. NOT KIDNAPPED.*

Texts pinged back at her.

Jesus Christ is Lord where are you?

Salvatore is all over our asses. We're trying to leave.

We have to get out. Some guys tried to break into my apartment last night but bldg. manager scared them off. I'm packing the diaper bag and our clothes right now.

S Grande knows the info we gave him about you was f'd up. We're dead if we don't get out.

The panic in their words was as palpable as if the letters pulsed with terror on the phone screen.

Kylie gave up trying to text and started a group call.

They all picked up.

"What the hell?"

"You gave us false information to tell Salvatore Grande? *We're in such deep shit!"*

"He's going to kill us. Or at least beat the shit out of us. Or make us give him all our money to make up for it, and we'll be *homeless."*

"Seriously, we didn't know what you told us was fake. We kept insisting it was right."

"Okay, okay!" Kylie yelled over their shrieks. *"I'm sorry.* I didn't know it was fake when I told you. Micah said that stuff to feed it to you, and then he took my phone so I couldn't warn you that it wasn't true. I *just* got my phone back. Like, *just now."*

"We are in *trouble,"* Rita told her with a tremble in her husky whisper. "We're getting the hell out of AC, but we don't have anywhere to go and no money to get out with."

Her girls, her gang, her only nets who had saved her from the bottomless pits of how far a young woman can fall in life, were desperate and in trouble.

Supposedly, Rachele and her mother were somewhere, but Kylie hadn't seen hide, golden hair, or evidence of life from them. They might be figments of Micah's imagination and Arthur's computer.

Her mother and sister were phantoms that disappeared from Kylie's fingers every time she reached for them.

They weren't real.

Rita, Priyanka, Alma, and Alma's kid needed Kylie like never before.

"I'm coming," Kylie told them, desperate to make it up to them. Alma had a *baby* who was in danger. She grabbed her purse and spilled out the last few stacks of cash that she'd grabbed from Salvatore Grande's desk. "I have money. I can get you money."

"Are you in Atlantic City?" begged Rita. "We need to leave *now*."

"I'm—" *Very far away.* "—not there."

"We need to get out of here *now*," Priyanka told her. "It's getting really dangerous."

"Okay, I, *um*—"

The door opened behind her. Micah's voice asked, "What are you doing?"

She looked up at him from sitting on the floor with useless wads of cash in her lap and desperate friends on the other side of the world. "It's my girls. They need this money to leave Atlantic City. This is all I've got. I don't know how to get it to them. I'm here. They're there. *I don't know how.*"

Micah closed the door and locked it. "I told you to stay off the phone."

"*But they're my friends.* I *can't* just abandon them. I need to take a plane to AC right now to go with them." The words felt right as they tumbled out of her mouth. "We were always in this together. I *owe* them. They're the only people in the world who give a damn about me, and Salvatore Grande is going to take *my lies* out of *their hide.*"

Micah strode across the small room and looked down at her, hot tears smearing her face, her hands cramping around the cell phone where her friends were begging for her help. "Oh, Kylie."

"I have to go."

"I need you here. We have a deal," he said.

"You don't need me. You've never needed me or even wanted me for anything other than to screw and leave."

He tilted his head. "That's never been true."

"They need me to help them. I'm *nothing* to you. You don't *care* about me. You don't *trust* me. I'm a tag-along and an easy lay, and that's all I am to you. *You don't need me."*

Pleading tumbled from her heart in a torrent.

She told him, "They're in trouble. Grande is after them. If I don't go there and help them, they might get killed but they'll definitely get hurt. *I have to be there.* They're all I've got left in the world. They've been there for me and helped me get a fake ID and a job so I wouldn't be homeless or in foster care or worse. If something happens to them, if Salvatore gets them, I'll have *no one* left. I'll be alone forever and ever. I can't abandon them. *I have to get to Atlantic City to help them!"*

21

SAVING THE AC GIRLS

MICAH

An easy lay.

Nothing to him.

The words smashed into Micah's chest like a sawed-off shotgun blast. "No. No, Kylie, it's not like that—"

But she wasn't listening to him. "I am absolutely nothing to you. They are *everything* to me. Please, help me get home. I don't care if Salvatore kills me or worse. At least I'll have saved *them.*"

The image of her stepping onto a plane that rose into the sky and flew out of sight over the horizon assailed him.

Gone.

Gone just like everyone else he'd ever cared about.

Gone, leaving him betrayed and alone.

He could let her go, if that's what she wanted, if that's what would actually make her happy.

But what she wanted was for her friends to be safe, and what *he* wanted was for Kylie to be safe.

Micah squatted beside where she huddled on the carpet with her few pathetic bundles of cash and plucked the phone from her fingers. She grabbed at it half-heartedly but was too defeated to stop him.

He asked her, "Can they get into your old apartment in AC?"

She nodded, tears streaking her cheeks with eyeliner shadows. "Rita has a key."

Micah said into the phone, "Go to Kylie's previous apartment. Someone will arrive with cash. Don't tell anyone where you're going. When you get the money, I expect you will leave AC and won't come back for at least six months. Just get out."

He thumbed the red dot on the screen.

Kylie shoved the wrapped bundles of money toward his feet. "Get this to them. I don't know how. I'll give you everything I have. *Just get it to them.*"

He wasn't going to take her money.

Micah pulled his phone from his hip pocket and touched a few spaces on the screen until it started ringing.

A man answered, "Hello? Micah?"

Ah, that mellow tone that sounded like a top-shelf gin fizz and someone playing the piano in the cigar-smoke haze. "Blaze, I need a favor that involves sixty thousand dollars."

Kylie was plucking at his trouser legs. "I only have about forty. I don't have sixty."

He covered the phone. "If your girls have twenty each, they should be okay for a while." Moving his hand, he said to Blaze, "Yeah, sixty grand. It's a drop-off in Atlantic City. Maybe seventy because one of them needs some extra. There's a kid involved. No, it's not mine," he said, preempting the inevitable question. "Where are you?"

"Chicago. Three hours by air. I'll charter." Blaze said. "I have that in my safe. It won't be a problem."

"I owe you one."

"*One?* Paris, last year. Cairo, the year before that. New York Christmas vacation, and senior year at Le Rosey."

Micah didn't mention the several times he'd bailed Blaze's ass out of a situation, but instead conceded, "Okay, I owe you *another* one. Take care." Micah looked back down at Kylie. "It's done. He's chartering a flight from Chicago to AC. He'll be on the ground in about three hours, at your apartment half an hour after that. They'll have the money, and they'll be able to leave. *They will be okay.*"

"I should go anyway," she said. "I should be with them when they need me."

"*I need you,*" Micah said, and his soul was as raw as flayed skin.

"No, you don't. *They* need me."

He rocked back and sat on the floor, the ship bobbing slightly under his butt and legs. A black hole occupied the place where the words usually were in his head. "Please don't go."

"Micah, if I can help them at all, if I can throw myself at Salvatore Grande to give them a shot at getting away, I should do that. *I did this to them.*"

"They'll be fine. Once they're outside of the greater Philadelphia and South Jersey area, Grande will lose interest. He doesn't want them hanging around as testimony that underlings can mess with him and get away with it. If they're living out their lives in some hick town in the Bible Belt, he won't care. They'll be dead to him. That's all he wants.

"*You don't know that.*"

"I know a lot about guys like Salvatore Grande."

Yeah, he hadn't meant to say *that.*

And Kylie was eyeing him with suspicion in her deep brown eyes. "Oh, *yeah?*"

"Yeah."

She raised both her dark eyebrows at him. "And you think you know more than *me,* the daughter of Joseph Merlino, Atlantic City *capo?*"

Micah muttered, "Yeah, because he wouldn't have told his *daughter* what he was doing."

He watched the fight rise in her and pink her cheeks. "Just because I'm a *girl* doesn't mean I'm *stupid.*"

"Oh, I *know* you're not stupid. I'm *counting* on it because I need you for every step of how we're going to rid ourselves of those damned paintings and get your mother and sister back. I'm just telling you what *he* wouldn't have done."

Kylie wound herself up, and her words were stiff jabs to his ribs. "I don't give a *damn* what you think and what my father would or wouldn't have done. I've been dealing with Salvatore Grande for years and know how to run *the goddamn garbage business.*"

"Right, and I'm counting on that, too," Micah told her. "If I thought you weren't competent and hard as nails when it comes to operations, I would lock you on this yacht or in Arthur's penthouse and play white knight for you. I'd go and rescue or kidnap back your mother and sister and dump them in your lap while you sit here, safe because I want nothing more in this life than for you to be *safe.* But you are smart and sharp and a pistol in a fight, and there's a better chance that your family will be safe if you're in the action. So even though it's killing me to put you in any kind of danger, *I need you.*"

"So I'm just a *business associate* to you," Kylie said, and she tossed her curls.

Oh God, she was ridiculously cute when she tossed her curls. He was goddamn lost.

Micah grabbed her wrist and pulled her into his lap, cradling her against his chest.

"Hey, whoa there, buddy!" she snarked at him. "Somebody might think we're more than just business associates."

"I have admired you from the moment I started watching you," he growled near her ear, and her lush body stilled in his arms. "You're loyal, and you're so brave. Confronting Salvatore Grande in his office and keeping your head about you was the most amazing thing I've ever seen. Your body, your fire, and your mouth dragged me in like I'd never seen a woman before, certainly never one like you. I want to keep you *safe*. When you're out of the room, I count the minutes until I find you again. When I'm with you, I'm straining not to take you in my arms and hold you again."

Kylie was staring up at him, ruby-lipsticked lips parted, and blinking with his every confession.

He said, "Your sister and mother are important to you, so they're important to me. I'm crashing whole operations because I want you to have your family if that's what you want. I know you're conflicted about whether to take care of your AC girls or your mom and sister, so I made it so both of them would be okay. When you want something, it becomes my dearest wish, and my whole world is turned upside down."

Her jaw had dropped so much that her mouth was more of an O now. Her voice was shaky as she whispered, *"Okay."*

"So I'm going to make sure your friends are safe, and I'm going to get your sister and your mother for you. I will remake the world to make you happy, Kylie, *Chiarina*, and keep you safe."

EVERYONE IS A MARK

KYLIE

TEMPTING
THE
BILLIONAIRE
Romantic Suspense with a Twist

USA TODAY BESTSELLING AUTHOR
BLAIR BABYLON

The first step to drawing the *Chekhovskaya* bratva out of hiding was to *lure* them.

That was Kylie's impression of the plan, anyway.

So Kylie's part of the first step of the plan involved her getting dressed up in a slinky gown that she'd purchased with Micah's credit card under the direction of the fantabulicious Countess Gen Finch-Hatten and then sitting still while a cosmetician came into their guest suite on the boat to do her hair and makeup.

Kylie watched the cosmetician's work closely. Somehow, when she was done, Kylie looked *high-class,* which she'd been trying to do when she'd been scamming in Atlantic City but never achieved.

Her hair fell in glossy curls but was swept into an updo with sparkly combs, and her face was glowy like she had no pores.

It was probably expensive makeup.

Kylie tilted her head and stared at the pretty girl in the mirror.

Her skin looked like it was made of pearls. That was amazing and a little alarming.

Yeah, those cosmetics must be *really expensive.*

Micah tipped the cosmetician and shooed her out of the cabin, and his scorching look made Kylie blush from her toes to her hairstyle.

"Later," he promised with a throaty growl. *"Later,* I will *ruin* all of this."

Micah had a box with a necklace and earrings that glittered like silver snow, and Kylie recognized *quality* diamonds. She'd seen enough of them while helping marks part with their cash. When he slid the heavy necklace around her throat, the cold metal felt like, for a night, she wasn't a trash kid who lived in an apartment with a rusty boiler and a stained sink.

And then there was another box she hadn't seen, and he wrapped her in a soft jacket that felt like silk.

The last paper shopping bag held a tiny clutch purse of quilted leather in dusky peach and the initials *YSL.*

She felt demure, or dainty, or something that Kylie Miller-slash-Chiarina Merlino had never felt before when Micah held her hand at twilight as she stepped down the gangplank from the ship onto the floating wooden sidewalk alongside. At the road, Micah opened the car door and handed her into the back seat of the limousine waiting for them in front of the Monaco Yacht Club.

Everything was a little shimmery, like the world was a little bit more okay and she was less afraid. Micah's words echoed in the sunny places between the buildings and on the platinum-capped wavelets of the sea.

I'm counting the minutes until I find you again.

My whole world is turned upside down.

His words wrapped her, held her, vibrated between them in the place where her hand was tucked in his elbow.

Kylie felt very quiet, holding the prismatic light with open hands, lest this feeling be startled into flying away.

Their limo was one among a fleet of limousines, and well-dressed people seemed to be stepping into each before they pulled away and other limos backed into their places.

"What's this thing tonight?" Kylie asked.

"Rain forest or something," Micah said with a shrug. "It doesn't matter. It's yet another charitable false front the wealthy use to shield their holdings and yet simultaneously display their vast wealth to each other like elephant seals flopping their nasal scrotums around and screaming to define their territories."

Outside Kylie's window, a middle-aged white dude in a tank top was listening to hip-hop as the orange and gold Bugatti convertible he drove screeched to a halt at a red light, and then he screamed until his face turned red at pedestrians in the crosswalk as the green walk signal blinked benignly.

Micah continued, "Considering that we're in Monaco, the charity is most likely associated with money laundering, too, which is why Monaco is the dirty pool where we're fishing for Russian organized crime rings like the *Chekhovskaya.*"

"This place doesn't look like a dirty pool," Kylie said, staring out the window at the glittering boutique jewelry and purse stores they passed.

Stores like these would be in the private high-roller area in the AC casinos, except that even the highest rollers probably wouldn't be admitted to these shops. Kylie had a sneaking suspicion that you had to be on a list or known by sight as worthy of crossing the thresholds of shops like those.

"I'm worried we won't be able to pull this off," she told Micah.

Micah wrapped his fingers around hers. "You can't con an honest person, right?"

You could, but you used a pity con instead of a greed con. "Yeah," Kylie said. "That's how you hooked me."

"And so, we're in luck because Monaco attracts thieves, gangsters, and criminals of all sorts. Everyone here is trying to steal something from someone, whether it's cheating on their taxes or selling drugs, guns, or people. In Monaco, everyone is a crook, which means everyone is a mark."

The limo turned a corner, and the nose tilted downhill. The street led to a long glass building like a turquoise and verdigris ocean wave as the sun dipped into the Mediterranean Sea beyond it.

The car turned into a circle in front, and Micah told her to wait while he walked around the back and offered her his hand as she stepped out. They walked into the Grimaldi Forum convention center together.

She shouldn't gawk. She shouldn't fall off her red-soled shoes and splat all over the marble floor.

Kylie just needed to con these snooty upper-class criminals instead of her usual middlebrow ones. It was fine.

At least she was adequately dressed for it.

Micah flashed an invitation at the security guys stationed at the doors, who read the QR hologram with a device and stood back for them to enter.

As they entered the convention center with three floors of overdressed guests, conversation noise bounced off glass walls that let the sunset in at one end of the building. Kylie asked Micah, "How did you get an invitation for this?"

Trumpets sounded.

A tuxedo-clad man and a softly pregnant blonde wearing a long gown appeared at the top of one of the staircases. A tiara wove in her hair, and every guest in the convention center turned toward them and applauded.

Micah whispered to her over the din. "Arthur called a friend of his to get us an invite. Hors d'oeuvres or dancing first?"

"Hors d'oeuvres. I'm famished."

Towers of canapés filled large tables along every available landing and nook in the convention center and were obsessively replenished by waitstaff.

The tiny pie crusts topped with roasted peaches and pastry cream globes shattered into flakes and caramel in Kylie's mouth.

She snagged a couple of cucumber rounds topped with cream cheese-piped flowers and salmon slivers. "These people don't fool ya. They feed ya."

"Indeed, and I would hope so, as tickets started at twenty-five grand."

Kylie carefully chewed and swallowed the most expensive appetizer she'd ever eaten in her life. The crisp cuke paired perfectly with the herbal cream cheese and mild sushi-grade fish. "Are you serious?"

"Quite."

She leaned over and whispered, "Couldn't we have just ransomed my sister and mom for that?"

"Probably not, and we aren't sure where they are."

"Right."

"If you've had enough grazing, perhaps some dancing?"

"Okay, but I'm coming back for those tiny waffles with chicken nuggets on them."

Kylie held up the front hem of her silk dress as they

climbed a curved staircase that seemed to spiral up toward the stars.

The dance floor was on the top floor of the convention center in a wing constructed from blue glass like an extension of the azure water outside the transparent walls and ceiling. The last streaks of sunset glowed in the darkening sky and reflected on the rippling surface of the Mediterranean Sea that rolled to the horizon.

Eight musicians played violins, bigger violins, cellos, and a standing bass fiddle. Kylie didn't recognize the song, but she hadn't listened to much classical music since her nonna died. No one else in the family listened to opera and Italian music like Nonna had because she'd been from the other side. The casinos played instrumental versions of classical songs, familiar and catchy but not interesting enough to distract people from gambling.

Micah flicked Kylie's hand, and she was spinning and then clasped in his arms. He smiled down at her, the teal flecks in his silver and aqua eyes catching the last of the sunlight outside the glass walls and ceiling like they were dancing under the sunset.

She asked him, "What color do you say your eyes are?"

He chuckled and looked over the heads of the other people dancing as he swayed with her in his arms. "I usually write down they're gray."

"But they're not gray."

"It depends on what I'm wearing."

"You must get that question a lot."

He shrugged. "It's a conversation opener. I have stock answers depending on who asks."

Kylie tried to follow his feet as they danced, but they ended up bobbing from side to side because she didn't know how to waltz or foxtrot or whatever he was doing.

She was in Micah's arms, and he kept smiling at her.

It felt kind of natural.

But like a toddler with a butterfly that alights on her finger, she decided to smash it. The only way to see if something was alive was to kill it.

"When we were on the yacht this afternoon—" Kylie began.

Micah tilted his head. "Mm-hmm?"

"You didn't mean what you said, right? I was just emo, and you cheered me up."

"I meant it," he said quietly, his voice low.

"But it was just because I was crying, right? Because I was manipulating you, just like I always do with guys in Atlantic City."

His soft smile turned a little more amused. "Is that what you think you were doing?"

"It's what I always do." Her strained voice sounded like she was forcing the words out.

Micah chuckled. "That is one interpretation of what happened, that you and your admitted conspirators presented me with a scenario where they were supposedly in jeopardy with time pressure and needed money, and you emotionally manipulated me into giving them ninety thousand dollars. Classic pity con. Huh. I guess that could also be an explanation."

The glass dome above them must have vanished, and the clammy sea air must have rushed in like a tsunami because Kylie's skin felt like a sheet of icy sweat had dropped over her. "Oh."

Micah's smile widened. "I don't believe that's what happened, even if it does fit the circumstances."

"But maybe I did."

Micah bent down to whisper in her ear, "You can't scare me off, *cara mia*."

"I wasn't trying to—"

"You're testing me to see if I'll abandon you. I won't, and you can't scare me by reframing what happened this afternoon."

"But you can't trust me," she said, her words fighting their way out of her throat. "You *don't* trust me."

He shrugged. "I don't share some operational details with you. That's different. You *can't* scare me off because *nothing* scares me."

"Oh, come on. How can *nothing* scare you? Or is this some riddle like 'no man *born of woman* can kill me,' and then the murderer was born by a C-section?" Her GED curriculum had reached Macbeth.

Micah shook his head. "*Nothing scares me.* I've seen worse. Things tire me, and some things need to be overcome or manipulated to get out alive, but nothing scares me, not even a woman who hints that she might be lying to swindle me out of small sums of money and doesn't realize she holds my heart."

No matter how the toddler tried to smash the butterfly, it still lived.

Micah whispered, "If you wanted me to give your friends ninety thousand dollars, you could have just said so, and I would have. I can't deny you anything, but that's not what happened. Instead, I saw a woman so loyal to her friends that she would walk into the line of fire for them, which in this case is Don Grande. You were going to give up finding your mother and sister because your friends needed you, even though your loyalty to both was tearing you apart, and *that* was tearing me apart. Maybe I would have said just about anything to make you stop crying, but instead, I told you what I didn't realize until it came out of my mouth. You amaze me, and I have lost my heart to you."

She held his hand more tightly, and her eyes burned. The Mediterranean Sea must have risen and flooded the Grimaldi Forum because everywhere she looked seemed underwater.

Micah pulled her over to the side and sat her down in a chair at one of the round tables ringing the dance floor, offering her a handkerchief from inside his tuxedo coat. "Don't cry," he whispered. "We have work to do tonight."

She hiccuped and pressed the cotton square underneath her eyes. Gray smudged the white cotton.

"And they're going to serve dinner," he told her. "I'm told it will be even better than the appetizers. And the dessert is supposed to be fantastic. There's a plated dessert and then buffet stations for different ones."

She laughed a little at his pep talk. "I—I didn't think I'd need to say this, but you have my heart, too."

Micah held both her hands in his, and she crushed the handkerchief. He leaned like he was going to whisper next to her ear, but his low voice growled, "God, I wish we were alone right now."

The slight smoke on his breath from the whiskey he'd had while she'd been busy scarfing canapés wafted over Kylie's throat.

She squeezed his hands. "There must be someplace here we could go."

Micah looked up at her, the aqua and turquoise shimmer in his eyes turning to blue fire. "We have things to do."

Kylie stared into the inferno in his eyes. "I didn't mean we should leave."

"I want to *show* you."

His wrist lying on her leg pulsed with his heartbeat. Kylie's dress constricted around her chest, and she sipped air to breathe. "Great. *Tonight.* When we get back to Twist's yacht. *But I want you now.*"

"I cannot deny you *anything.*" He stood and pulled Kylie to her feet with their linked hands, and he looked around the ballroom, the people dancing, and the edges of the room that seemed to end in a cliff overlooking the darkening sea beyond the glass walls and ceiling.

Micah said, "Come with me."

23

UNDER THE STARS

MICAH

TEMPTING THE **BILLIONAIRE**

Romantic Suspense with a Twist

USA TODAY BESTSELLING AUTHOR
BLAIR BABYLON

Desire vibrated through Micah as he broke through the crowd packed into the Grimaldi Forum, holding Kylie's hand behind him. His racing heart pounded blood through his veins, and the collar of his tuxedo shirt squeezed his throat. He stuck a finger in his collar and unbuttoned it behind his tie.

There must be some way to get up there.

The ballroom was on the top floor. Maxence and Dree had obviously been helicoptered in and appeared at the top of this staircase for their entrance, so he just needed—

A door.

In a back corner of the ballroom, a short hallway led away from the glassed-in area, but catering staff were walking right past it for the wider one with swinging doors at the end.

Micah led Kylie to it, and with just a quick kneel to feel the tumblers in the doorknob with two specialized tools from the inside of his tuxedo jacket, they found a utilitarian cement stairwell leading up.

The door banged closed behind them, and the crowd

noise that had bellowed around them all night and classical musicians playing Mendelssohn's "Octet in E-flat Major" shut off with a click.

Micah's ears whined as he wheeled Kylie around, and she climbed one stair before he pressed her back against the wall and kissed her, his mouth roving over hers and touching her throat and collarbones left bare in that slip of a dress with nothing but spaghetti straps that he could have snapped with one swift yank.

No, he admonished himself. He had to be gentle. He had to be careful.

He couldn't wreck her *yet.*

But he had to have her.

A light scent like flowers rose from her skin, and he inhaled through his nose, his back bowing as he breathed, his heart pounding, his body swelling with violent desire.

His hands were filled with her curves, his thumbs teasing her breasts through the silk of her dress and his palms grasping the rounds of her ass. Her breath quickened, and she made a little sound in her throat.

His waistband loosened, and her fingers tickled against his stomach.

Micah broke off the kiss, whispering, *"Not here,"* to her.

Kylie's whimper shot lust like fire through his flesh.

"Upstairs. *Come on.*"

He buttoned the waistband of his pants—no cummerbund, he didn't like them—and he pulled Kylie up the stairs to the door to the top, twisted the knob, and they were on the roof under the stars with the waves of the Mediterranean lapping at the shore just beyond.

Autumn air chilled Micah's face. He whipped off his jacket and wrapped it around Kylie's shoulders as he hurried her around the stairwell egress, away from the red pinpricks and white floodlights of the helicopter landing pad.

The back side of the stairwell access blocked the lights, and the glow of Monaco around the convention center and the stars above them traced pale silver lines over Kylie's form. Fresh salt air from the sea wove through his hair, pulling the overheated humidity off him.

Kylie clutched his tuxedo coat around her, peering through the darkness and then up at the stars. "Oh, this is beautiful."

Her words stood in his mind for a second before his desire and chaos blew them away. His need for her felt like air hunger when swimming frantically for the surface of the ocean, and he was on her again, his mouth on her throat and shoulders, his hands on her breasts and hips, sweeping his fingers and palms over her skin and curves to make her as wild as he was.

Her gasps and moans drove him higher, and she was trying to unbutton his trousers as he gathered her skirt above her hips. He found her skin, touching and stroking her as his mouth moved on hers, and then she gasped as his thumb and fingers touched her, stroked her, deeper until her hips moved on his hand and her fingernails scratched at the thin fabric of his shirt.

Shoving and gripping bared her to him, and Micah attempted to snatch at his wallet for a condom but she was holding him, crying in his ear, "Please, now, *please now*."

"I have to get a—"

"Please, Micah."

"I have—"

"I need—*please, Micah.*"

And the words were gone, and his thoughts were gone, and he thrust up inside her, her leg wrapped around his hips, bare and naked and skin-to-skin inside, a *heat* and friction that left him gasping like a virgin and squeezing his eyes shut and crushing her against him. Mindless thrusting, his body an animal taking her, forcing her hips down as he shoved himself up and into her and felt her writhe and heat and wriggle while she was pinned on his cock.

Her body pulsed around him, a fluttering and rhythmic wave that drew his response out of him, a moment of blindness and bliss suspended in time, and then the pounding in his temples and his heart and his balls at the instant of his release.

Inside her.

Deep inside her.

A primal instinct kept him there, her limbs locked around him, a selfish demon that demanded his body take her, pump into her, *possess her.*

For long moments, *too long,* Micah was lost in the waves of orgasm, and then his breath sounded in his head and his lungs, and then he realized what he'd done. *"Kylie, I didn't—"*

She was panting and clinging to his shoulder, the breeze jostling her dark curls that bled into the night.

"Kylie."

"Oh my God, *yes.* Do you even have to ask? I think I had an *aneurysm.*"

He backed away from her, using a handkerchief to dry himself and arranging his clothes as he confessed, "I wasn't wearing a condom. *I'm sorry.* I couldn't think straight. You grabbed me, you wanted, and I didn't *think.* We can get one of those pills. The morning after ones. I can have it delivered to the yacht as soon as we get there."

"Micah, it's *fine,"* Kylie said, tugging the skirt of her gown down her hips and legs and shimmying to rearrange her body inside. "I get the Depo shot. I got one just a couple weeks before I met you. It's almost two months until the next one's due. I'm not running around Atlantic City *fertile*. I mean, *eek*."

"Oh, okay. It won't happen again."

Disappointment warred with the relief that should have run through him but was a void.

Rather than deal with that, he pushed Kylie back against the wall and kissed her again, his mouth on hers, his body holding hers, stealing a moment before they went back inside to the party.

She melted against him, her arms winding around his neck.

But the moment ended when she shivered in his arms. "Are you cold?"

"It's a little breezy on this roof."

"Come on. There are people in there we need to talk to. Arthur's friend has arranged several chance meetings where we'll be seen talking to international criminals."

Micah's eyes had adjusted to the glow from Monaco around the Grimaldi Forum and the sky above the sea.

Kylie smiled serenely under the stars. "Oh, lovely. Just like Sunday dinner at Nonna's after Mass. Lead on."

24

DASHA BUTORIN
MICAH

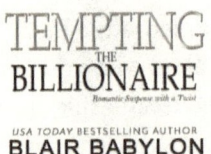

The languid aftereffects of Kylie in his arms quenched the irritable energy in Micah's brain.

Her light hand wrapped under his elbow, and he marveled at how beautifully she was still made up, not a wrinkle in her gown or a curl out of place as she smiled, whereas he felt windblown and like he'd finished an exhilarating race.

And won.

The time was seven thirty-five, as planned, and they strolled through the main lobby, ostensibly heading for the appetizer buffets again.

A passing woman wearing a black satin dress caught Micah's other arm. She said to him in Russian, "Micah Shine! Good Lord and all the good saints, I haven't seen you since senior year at Le Rosey. It's been too long. Where *have* you been hiding yourself?"

"Mostly America, over in California. So good to see you." Cheek kisses like the French, and then Micah switched to English to introduce Kylie. "Kylie, *cara mia,* this is my school chum, Dasha Butorin. She was two years behind me." He turned back. "How is your sister Sofiya?"

"She's good, really good," Dasha said. "Married with two kids. She never gets to see them because she's busy with *the family business*. You know she took over a while ago."

"I heard, and it's great that she's doing so well. I'm not surprised. She always had a head for business."

"I'll tell her you asked after her." Dasha bent sideways and grinned at Kylie. "And who's this?"

Micah touched the fragile silk dress on Kylie's back and ushered her forward. "Kylie and I have been seeing each other for quite some time. She's from *an old family* in Sicily. They should be sending their future generations to Le Rosey for the connections."

Maxence had outdone himself with this arranged meeting. The Butorin family's influence in the *Solntsevskaya* bratva waxed and waned depending on which of their leaders had been murdered or jailed lately, like most connected families in most Russian bratvas, but Dasha Butorin was known as an up-and-comer.

And his old friend Sofiya Butorin was in charge, which he wasn't pleased to hear. Micah would have preferred to ruin someone like Sergey Butorin.

Dasha smiled at Kylie, her blood-red lips curving like a sickle. "So nice to meet you. I'm surprised we haven't met at one of these various things. My family hasn't done much business with the Sicilian side. We deal mostly with people from around Naples, but it's always nice to make connections, as Micah noted." She winked. *"Oh,* I heard that Micah has a most *interesting item* he's acquired."

Micah raised one eyebrow. "Maybe you heard right. Maybe you heard I have two of them."

"*Oh, really?*" Dasha tucked her hand under Micah's other arm, smiling conspiratorially across his chest at Kylie. "Let's take a turn around the room and discuss said items, shall we?"

That whole conversation was a study in the subtleties of the criminal underworld, and Micah always understood far more of it than he ever let on.

Instead, he smiled back at Dasha Butorin as they discussed taboo topics in code.

Dasha said, "I heard an Old Master might be in play."

"You heard right," Micah said. "And again, *both.*"

"Two Old Masters?" a man said, turning toward them. "Did I hear someone discussing art?"

"Why, yes," Dasha cried, and Micah detected artifice. "Micah, you remember Anatoly Ostrovsky from a few years ahead of us at Le Rosey? He's heading the *Chekhovskaya* people now."

The name *Chekhovskaya* pinged warning bells. Though the word ostensibly meant something as innocuous as *from the Chekhov region,* a powerful Russian bratva had taken that name as their own, just like the Butorins had for the *Solntsevskaya bratva.*

While the *Chekhovskaya bratva* rang alarms in his head, the name Anatoly Ostrovsky did not.

Micah remembered a lot about what his mother and father had talked about at night, even though he'd been a child. He'd been *right there* at the kitchen island doing homework while his mother washed up and his father stood at the back door, blowing cigarette smoke outside.

They'd meant for Micah to hear. He was the oldest son and the heir apparent to an empire that seemed to be composed of a few pizza joints and a recycling collection business. How such modest businesses supported an eight thousand square foot palazzo with a domestic staff of five on the water in Middletown, New Jersey was a mystery.

At ten years old, he'd been three years away from beginning to pursue minor errands. He'd already walked down the sidewalk with his father, talking to people, watching, and learning. The Mafia is an apprenticeship. There is no bachelor's degree in organized crime.

The name Anatoly Ostrovsky didn't ring Micah's memory bells, which meant Ostrovsky had taken power sometime in the last thirteen years. He was also an important name in the dossiers Arthur had given him to read and memorize, which *did* set off alarms.

Micah grinned. *"Anatoly!* Of course, I remember you and your cousin who was a year behind us at Le Rosey. How is Timur?"

Anatoly Ostrovsky shrugged one shoulder, and his boxy-cut tuxedo rippled the dark gray fabric. "Trusted."

"Excellent. May I introduce Kylie Miller, from *an old Sicilian family.* We've been seeing each other for a while."

Kylie held out her hand to shake. "Pleased to meet you."

Ostrovsky rotated her hand and brushed his lips absently over her knuckles before he dropped it. *"Kylie Miller,* huh? Doesn't sound Sicilian."

Micah hesitated.

Nope. No hesitations. *Those were death.*

The words were *there* in his head and Micah reached for them, but Kylie had already touched her raven-wing curls and batted her dark eyes at the Russian, asking, "Why advertise?"

Ostrovsky seemed to get it with an upside-down smile and vague glance around, and he nodded. "Yeah, why give it away?"

"Exactly," Kylie said, smiling.

The goddamned perfect pinch-hit. This woman was like a third hand in a knife fight.

"If somebody knows who you are, they *know*," Anatoly Ostrovsky commented.

Kylie quipped, "And if they don't know why the *Chekhovskaya* are important, why enlighten them? They might be competition, or they might be trouble."

Just damned perfect.

Anatoly turned to Micah. "I like this girl. She thinks like a Sicilian, that's for sure."

Micah smiled down at Kylie, at her perfect mouth he wanted to ravage and her perfect wit he could count on. "I like her, too."

She smiled up at him, a naughty sparkle in her dark eyes. A gentle breeze of warmth feathered Micah's skin to his feet.

Dasha Butorin winked at Micah and wandered into the crowd, having done her job.

"But you said something about Old Master art," Ostrovsky said to Micah, his body language looser. *Yes, the mark was taking the bait.* "What kind of Old Master?"

"As with Kylie," Micah said, "sometimes names are distracting."

"But as with me," Ostrovsky said, "would I know the names?"

Micah winked at him. "If you took Master Levecque's Art Investing class senior year, you would know one of them. The other, everyone knows."

Anatoly Ostrovsky made an *I'm-thinking* face with that exaggerated upside-down smile. "Interesting. Displayable?"

"Only privately," Micah told him.

"Still interesting," Ostrovsky said.

Excellent. Micah turned toward him.

Ostrovsky seemed to be holding his breath.

Micah said, "One of them will shake to their core any viewer who recognizes it. I nearly gasped, but I was busy at the time."

Micah was so close to Anatoly that he saw the older man's pupils expand in his eyes as if he were sexually aroused. *"Intriguing.* Will someone try to kill me to get it?"

"Oh, yes."

Ostrovsky probably was popping a chubby at the thought of having something so singular that it would evoke a murderous response from his friends.

"Excellent. What are bids thus far?"

"Couldn't say."

"Yeah, that's the business."

Micah fanned the air with his hand like he was drawing bids toward himself, but he said, "As much as I'm aware of the *value* to any collector, I'm also interested in the value to all humanity. Its previous residence was not in an appropriately controlled climate. The owner *smoked* in the room with it."

"Oh, no," Ostrovsky said.

Micah said, "I'm afraid so. He wasn't the *best* sort of person."

"I would *never,"* Ostrovsky assured him.

Micah leaned toward Ostrovsky as if he were telling him a secret. "I am absolutely sincere in saying that I would make a disposal decision based on assurances *and evidence* that they would be properly preserved for the future."

"You are man of great morals."

"No, I'm not. That's why I have the paintings," Micah said.

Ostrovsky laughed.

"But it is part of the decision. The winning bid will

include such assurances that they will be properly preserved for the future."

"I have friend who works at Hermitage Museum in St. Petersburg. She can direct preservation and proper display, but discreetly."

Micah raised his eyebrows and grinned. "I'll bet she's an endless supply of artistic treasures."

Ostrovsky laughed and pointed at Micah, for he had scored a point.

During Putin's kleptocracy, The Hermitage and Russia's other museums were thought to have lost half their collections from employees selling off the treasures to get enough money to live. The graft was just more collateral damage from not paying citizens an honest wage and concentrating wealth in the hands of people who have no morals and would squirrel away the world's treasures because they wanted to tell their friends they *owned* them.

"I'd be interested in seeing the accommodations for the secure transportation and preservation of any such artwork," Micah told him.

Ostrovsky nodded as if only the wise would make such a request. "I would be pleased to show you our facilities. We have warehouse in France just outside of the principality. We would store items there until suitable museum-quality transportation could be arranged. You could inspect within a few days."

And they were in.

"Splendid," Micah said, and they moved apart.

Anatoly Ostrovsky was only the first Russian oligarch or organized crime boss they met that night. Not only would stopping with Anatoly provoke suspicions, but Micah had two piping hot paintings that he didn't want to get caught with. He'd been an upstanding citizen for several years and didn't plan to run Shine Industries from prison.

Also, Arthur Finch-Hatten expected a full report on everyone Micah met, what they'd talked about, and any intelligence he could glean from that encounter.

And his other project required progress soon.

Sometimes the people Micah was working for and the ones he was betraying tangled in his head.

Another Russian oligarch touched Micah's arm, and they also had a conversation about certain Old Master paintings that may or may not be on the auction block and the location of his warehouses just outside the borders of Monaco. Land inside Monaco was at such a premium that very little was used for storage or distribution, not when a truck could drive a mile and a half and exit the imaginary lines that divided the world into income-tax-payers and tax-dodgers.

An Italian businessman and his companion approached them, noting whom Micah had been talking to and making an effort to introduce himself. They were Domenico Mallardo and his much younger mistress, who wasn't significant enough to be named and didn't seem to care or listen.

Micah said, "Mallardo, from around Giugliano in Napoli, correct? A pleasure."

"Yeah," Mallardo said. "I'm always interested in art. You should keep my number. Gia, give his girl your number, and she can give it to Mr. Shine."

From Arthur's dossiers, Micah knew Domenico Mallardo was the don of the Mallardo clan of the *Secondigliano* Alliance, a major branch of the Naples Camorra Mafia, which reportedly controlled most of the drugs sold in Spain, the Netherlands, and Northern Italy, among other businesses. Domenico's soft cheeks and curly dark hair looked like the picture in Arthur's file from when he'd been arrested for masterminding a triple murder to knock out the leadership of a rival clan, but he'd escaped prison from a hospital in his hometown.

They moved through the crowd, stopping at the appetizer tables so Kylie could try the cracker-sized waffles topped with a shaving of deep-fried chicken and a swirl of maple butter. Her surprised grin made Micah laugh and stack a plate with three more as the crowd drained toward the dining tables for the plated supper.

As he held the plate out to Kylie, who took one and bit into it with an eyeroll of ecstasy, Micah heard a man's voice speak in a New York accent. "I heard you're Micah Shine."

The voice stirred memories, but the rasp from fifteen more years of cigarettes was new.

Not a tremor of fear passed through Micah, just anger.

He turned with the mildest of smiles on his face, but he took half a step to stand between Kylie and the man he knew he would be facing. "Who's asking?"

The man was holding a highball glass of amber liquid in one hand that Micah knew would be Irish whiskey. His hair was dark gray, whereas Micah remembered him with only a touch of iron at his temples. The man peered at Micah and asked, "Do I know you?"

Micah handed off the plate of hors d'oeuvres to Kylie and held out his perfectly dry hand. "I don't believe I've had the pleasure."

"Vincent Genovese," the man said. "Of New York."

Anger turned to rage turned to cut-crystal intent in Micah's head. "Of course, I should have realized. It's a pleasure to finally meet you. Everyone says you're a good man to know."

"Yeah, thank you, thank you," Genovese said, turning his face aside with a small smile. "It's nice of them to say that."

"Are you enjoying the event? It is for such a good cause."

"Yeah, the cause. I heard you were talking to Domenico Mallardo about some art."

"He's a knowledgeable man."

"Yeah, he's knowledgeable. I got some knowledge about art, too, and I'm willing to bid double whatever he did. As a matter of fact, I'd be much obliged if you would sell it to me."

Micah touched his stomach as if surprised. "I had no idea that you might be interested, or else I would have tried to contact someone in your organization immediately. Your commitment to art is legendary. Placing one of these pieces with you would be an honor."

"Thank you, thank you again," Genovese said. "That's real nice of you to say."

Real Mafia men were not half-enraged bullies snarling and shoving their way through a territory. Dons and capos were unfailingly polite to other men because the wrong word or perceived rudeness could mean the deaths of dozens of people in their organization.

Genovese said, "I'll have my girl give her number to your girl here, and then we can contact each other."

Micah turned his head slightly to talk to Kylie. "My love, if you would be so good."

Vincent Genovese gestured with his chin at the dark-haired woman who'd stepped out from his shadow. "Alessia, give her your number."

Micah was calculating fast in his head. To do reconnaissance for finding Kylie's sister and mother, they needed to get inside the warehouse of the *Chekhovskaya* bratva, but there really was no mandate to sell Anatoly Ostrovsky both of the paintings or even one. If Kylie's family wasn't being held at the warehouse, they had no reason to continue to look there. Micah could dispose of those paintings in any way he wanted.

Selling one of Salvatore Grande's paintings to Vincent Genovese, the New York Mafia Don whom Grande was at war with, would inflame the tensions to the point where both organizations might be wiped out.

Just as long as Vincent Genovese didn't figure out why Micah looked so familiar.

Because the last time Genovese had seen him, Micah had been a platinum-blond ten-year-old.

HALF-SICILIAN

KYLIE

ylie noticed that Micah was a little bit twitchier than usual during dinner.

He wasn't flinching away from things. If anything, when a waiter dropped a tray full of wine glasses, Micah instantly had his hand on Kylie's shoulder and pressed her down, but he was starting to stand up. When Kylie lost her grip on her fork, it bounced off her plate and he caught it before it touched her lap, and then he fed her the bite of lobster without letting even a drop of the melted butter hit the silver silk of her dress.

The alertness looked like he was itching to go into battle.

As a result, Micah was a little more *on* that night, a little more expressive and sharp, and he had all ten people at their round table laughing at his jokes and telling him stories about themselves.

An hour later, Kylie was pretty sure that most of the people at the table assumed they were all best friends and would go on vacation together for the rest of their lives.

While the waiters were clearing the supper plates in anticipation of serving dessert, Kylie realized that she'd been drinking champagne and water all night and needed to avail herself of the ladies' room. As she minced away, one of the other guys at the table was enthusiastically telling Micah about a business deal he'd made in China and offering to cut Micah in. From his abject enthusiasm, any deal that came Micah's way would be to the other guy's detriment.

Ah, a self-con. Not an easy thing to watch.

After utilizing the ladies', Kylie was striding out the swinging door and looking over the tiled expanse of tables to make her way back to Micah when she spied Alessia, the rather young woman who'd been hanging on the elbow of Micah's last conquest before dinner, walking very quickly while a man was talking to her. The guy's paunch had certainly taken forty or more years to acquire, and Kylie could practically smell his hair oil from across the room.

He grabbed the young woman's elbow.

Alessia jerked her arm, but the guy wouldn't let go. His smarmy leer was revolting, and when he spoke, Alessia's head bobbed back like he had fish breath or was spitting his consonants.

Kylie was already trotting toward the other woman as she called out, "Hey, Alessia! I heard you were here. I've been looking for you all over."

Alessia turned, her dark eyes shining with fear.

Kylie marched straight toward her, jammed herself between Alessia and the molester dude, and then led Alessia toward the ladies' room, keeping up a constant stream of patter about common friends who didn't exist the whole way.

Once inside the bathroom, Alessia blew out a breath she'd evidently been holding and swore a blue streak that would have impressed a professional golfer. "I was trying not to make a scene, but I could not get away from him."

Kylie patted her on the back. "Are you okay?"

"That was Tommaso Maisto. He's from Providence and in the same business as my dad." Alessia shot a squinty glance at Kylie, indicating the Mafia.

"Oh! Vincent Genovese is your *dad!* I thought you guys were—"

"Dear God, *no.* He's my *father.* His *comare* broke up with him last year and moved to Greece, so I have to come to these networking events with him to play secretary."

"Wow. I don't think my father would have done that. So, the guy accosting you doesn't know who *your father* is or something?"

"Oh, he *knows.* The Maistos think they should be given an equal seat at the table as the Genovese family, even though, you know, *Providence.*"

"Yeah, I'm from New Jersey. Those Rhode Island people come down the shore to our beaches and think they own the place."

"*Right?* Tommaso thinks one way to move up to the big leagues is to force *me* into an arranged marriage with him. Evidently, that's how they did it back in the old days, meaning the early two-thousands. A car would drive up, and a girl would be snatched and driven to a church, where a Mafia priest would conduct the rite of matrimony even though the girl was crying and trying to get away. And you know, we're Italian, so that was that."

"And he was trying to kidnap you from *here?* We're in Monaco."

"We're *this close* to Italy." Alessia held her fingers a tiny bit apart and peered through them at Kylie. "You know there's got to be a priest right over the border in Italy who would probably do it."

Kylie took a towel from the washroom attendant and gave it to Alessia. "I'm Sicilian. I get it."

She had heard of those kidnapping-marriages for power and dynasty reasons from some of her aunts. Also, sometimes when a girl's father got himself deep in gambling debt to some Cosa Nostra goon, he offered his daughter in marriage to pay off the debt.

"I thought you might be Sicilian. You look Sicilian," Alessia said to Kylie, dabbing her eyes.

"I'm half, but I take after my father's side. I don't look like my mother at *all*. My dad was Sicilian, and I was raised mostly with my nonna and his relatives."

She nodded. "Italian genes are strong. I'm Napolitano, and look at this black hair and eyes."

"Yeah, sometimes. My sister, Rachele, has light brown hair and hazel eyes. She takes a lot after my mom's side. I never really met any of them."

Alessia finger-combed her black curls in the mirror. "I wish I'd gotten some of those recessive Northern Italian genes. When I color my hair lighter, it doesn't look right. The Italian genes are just too strong."

"But they don't have to be. Micah, the guy I've been seeing for a while," Kylie said, trying out that phrase but finding it awkward, "is half Sicilian, too."

"No," Alessia said, turning to Kylie with wide-shocked eyes. "He has light hair and blue eyes, right?"

"His eyes are gray and blue, and there's some green in there. He takes after his mom, who was Norwegian."

"Half Norwegian, half Sicilian, there's a combination you don't hear about every day."

"It explains why he's so tall, too. It's the Norwegian."

Alessia grinned. "I noticed."

Kylie snickered.

"But he's so light. What did your family say when you brought him home?"

"My dad isn't around anymore, so it wasn't much of a problem."

Alessia winced. "Oh, I'm sorry."

"It was a while ago. I'm okay. Hey, do you need an escort back to your seat so that Tommaso creeper doesn't try to carry you off again?"

"If you wouldn't mind. I'll drag my dad around with me for the rest of the night so Tommaso will keep his distance, and then I'll bet my dad will make some discreet inquiries about what hotel Tommaso Maisto is staying in and beat the living shit out of him tomorrow."

"Okay," Kylie said. "As long as that's settled."

After delivering Alessia back to her father with much hugging and assurances that Alessia was okay to alert her dad that something serious had happened, Kylie wandered back to Micah.

He slid his arm around the back of her chair. "Everything okay?"

"Sure. Got to talking with a friend."

He smiled and kissed her on her temple, and then the table went back to talking about the best places to take honeymoons.

Kylie wondered how the heck that conversation had come up.

WHERE THE WRITER ANTON CHEKHOV IS BURIED

MICAH

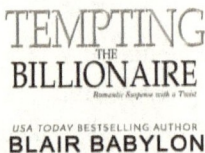

TEMPTING
THE
BILLIONAIRE
Romantic Suspense with a Twist

USA TODAY BESTSELLING AUTHOR
BLAIR BABYLON

T he next morning, the wind skimmed over the water of the marina, topping the glistening wavelets with foam.

Micah and Kylie sat on the main deck in a living room with an enormous TV on one wall fronted with couches and chairs. The back of the deck was open to the Mediterranean air, fresh with the scents of saltwater and sunshine. The other sides of the deck had been enclosed for the winter with glass, but the weather was still temperate enough for the rear to be left open.

Micah was reading a book he'd gleaned from Twist's library on the economic effects of the coming NFT and cryptocurrency crash because people were going to realize that owning a blockchain meant nothing, but people still hadn't realized stocks and options were essentially as ephemeral and herd-mentality as digital assets, either.

Kylie was working on something on a tablet. When Micah sneaked a glance, it appeared to be Shakespeare, and then he felt like a slacker for reading economic handwaving.

The sea lapped at the sides of the boat. Kylie sighed and

adjusted her curvy legs on her deck chair, and Micah could have lived there forever.

Maybe on his own yacht, once the world was a better place.

Kylie jumped and checked her phone, tapping the screen. "Hello? Oh, sure. Here he is." She held out the phone to Micah. "It's Anatoly Ostrovsky. Why doesn't he call your phone?"

Because plausible deniability is a thing. "Thank you, *cara mia.*" He took the phone. "Hello?"

"Do we have deal?" Ostrovsky asked.

"I appreciate your assurances, and we have a deal contingent upon seeing your operation for myself."

"Excellent. A car will pick you up to inspect warehouse and transportation two days from now, Monday, at ten o'clock that morning."

"I must insist I will drive myself."

"What, you don't trust—"

"A matter of policy."

"I will text address to this phone at nine o'clock that morning and meet you at ten. Acceptable?"

"Absolutely."

"Good doing business with you." Ostrovsky hung up.

Micah handed Kylie's phone back to her.

Twist yelled from the back of the deck, having stuck his head in from the hallway. "That was it, huh?"

Micah twisted in his deck chair. "Yeah. Did you get it?"

"Of course. I love it when they try to keep it short, like we need seven whole seconds to trace a call anymore. I traced it in something more like seven nanoseconds."

Micah stood and bent to kiss Kylie, his lips lingering on hers for a few seconds before he had to follow Twist back to his Evil Mastermind Lair.

Twist led Micah down a spiral staircase from the living room deck to his enclosed office on the waterline level below.

The deck bobbed gently under Micah's feet as he squinted in the bright Mediterranean sunshine. On the mountains surrounding the harbor of Port Hercule, rich earth-hued buildings and glass skyscrapers packed the cliff faces like careful stacks of blocks, and veil-like clouds streaked the cobalt sky above. The geography funneled the noise from the streets crowded with pedestrians, supercars, and delivery trucks, the roar sliding down the hills and trickling into the quiet of the sea.

They ducked in a door on the main deck at the stern of the boat.

The computer screen array in the blacked-out room dazzled Micah's sun-adapted vision, and he stood, blinking, while Twist dumped himself into the office chair in front of the keyboard.

The screens began to flicker and change.

Twist said, "So it looks like the call was made from his *comare's* phone, which was located at the Hotel de Paris Monte-Carlo down by the casino."

Micah chuckled. *"Comare,* huh? Did you google Mafia slang or somethin'?" he asked when he could finally see in the darkened room.

"Yeah, I did. When I use Mafia slang, your New York accent comes back for a minute. You might want to watch that if you're hiding it."

That was a problem. Micah should be careful to be consistent.

Twist continued, "But more importantly, my snooper found which Wi-Fi node the phone was logged into and therefore what hotel room Ostrovsky is in. The room was rented by a company called Novodevichy Cemetery, Inc. Does that ring a bell?"

The bells in Micah's head had been busy lately. "Novodevichy Cemetery is where the author Anton *Chekhov* is buried. Ostrovsky's bratva is from the *Chekhov* region, the *Chekhovskaya*." Micah shook his head. "Novodevichy Cemetery is where Chekhov, or the *Chekhovskaya*, are *buried* or *hidden*."

Twist looked up at Micah, pale light from the screens reflecting on the far side of his face. "And you knew where the author Anton Chekhov is buried, how?"

Micah shrugged. "The actual Novodevichy Cemetery is in the middle of Moscow. Yeltsin, Prokofiev, and thousands of other poets and politicians are buried there. I paid my respects to a few artists when I was in high school when I went home with a Russian friend for a month over summer break."

"And that friend was?" Twist asked. His suspicious squint was accusing.

Micah's shrug and look-around felt a little too wiseguy for comfort. "Sofiya Butorin."

Twist laughed out loud. "I didn't know you hung out with the bratva kids."

"I hung out with everybody. That was the summer when my Russian finally got fluent."

"Funny that you hung out with *Sofiya* Butorin in high school, and we're looking for a *Sofia* who is Kylie's mother."

"They're spelled differently, and they would be vastly different ages. Probably twenty years or more." He stressed the final syllable of Sofiya to differentiate between the two spellings as he said, "Sofi-*ya* Butorin is a year older than we are."

Accounting for how old Micah was supposed to be.

In reality, Sofiya had been three years older than Micah when he'd visited her family's Moscow penthouse, their Crimean dacha, and her bedroom that summer, but Micah had been lying about his age since he was eleven. Luckily, Micah had grown early for his actual age, though it appeared to be a year later than everyone else in his grade.

Micah continued, "The target's spelling is Sofia-with-an-I, the usual Italian spelling, though Sofi-*ya* had an aunt in Moscow who spelled it like Sofia-with-an-I. It's an alternate Russian spelling, too. But Kylie assures me she's a hundred percent Sicilian."

Twist had lost interest and turned back to his computer. "Right, okay. So, let's search Novodevichy Cemetery, Inc. and get more information on what we're dealing with here." Results from Google and a dark-web browser scrolled up the screens. "The company owns or rents several properties around Monaco. Here's a warehouse that looks promising. Let's pull up recent satellite imagery, and yep, significantly increased activity over the last two days. Looks like air conditioning and other climate control trucks here and here." Twist pointed. "What else would we be looking for?"

"Art professionals, specialized packing equipment."

Twist started clicking on cars. Imaging software read the license plates on the satellite images and searched public databases. "Here's one registered to an art historian associated with the Louvre in Paris. This car is registered to a curator at the New National Museum of Monaco, which is visual arts. I believe we have a hit."

Micah nodded. "That's where they're planning to take the painting, anyway. I don't know. My intelligence contact said the *Chekhovskaya* bratva had Rachele and Sofia, but I don't like that we haven't seen them or have any direct evidence that they're in France right now. And even when I get in there, Ostrovsky isn't going to show me their climate-controlled art storage facilities and then be like, 'Ignore the wretched prisoners in the barred cell.' What else can we hack while we're waiting forty-eight hours for me to get in there?"

Twist chuckled. "Oh, let me work on that. And while I'm doing that, you might want to check with your friends who also hack *or whatever* and see what else they can dig up. They were very helpful when Max was trying to get Dree back from the Sokolovs."

Yeah, Micah needed to contact Arthur Finch-Hatton and call in the cannons. There was no reason to walk into that warehouse with guns blazing if Kylie's mother and sister weren't there.

Arthur might be able to determine whether Kylie's family was being held hostage there or not, or maybe he could give Micah and Twist some toys so they could find out.

COFFEE AND PASTRY AT THE PORT DE FONTVIEILLE IN MONACO

MICAH

E arly the next morning, the sunlight painted the sky peach and gold, but the sun hadn't breached the eastward mountains.

Micah walked along the twilight pier of the Port de Fontvieille, a separate harbor less than half a mile away from Port Hercule where Twist's yacht was moored. He carried a brown briefcase of unremarkable character, midrange in expense, medium in color, and median in size. Probably a hundred men within half a mile were carrying something so similar as to seem identical.

At a small café across the street from the restless water, Micah sat at a table in a far corner, ordering a café au lait and a raspberry pastry. He sipped the coffee, but the pastry lay untouched until another unusually tall man, black of hair and gray of eye, sat next to him with his back against the other wall.

As Arthur Finch-Hatton unbuttoned his navy-blue suit jacket and sat in the other chair, he reached wide as he set his own nondescript brown briefcase on the ground, placing it between Micah's bag and Micah's leg.

Once Arthur had made the drop, Micah went ahead and ate the Danish. The pastry sitting on the table was his signal to Arthur that Micah hadn't been followed and it was safe to approach. If Micah had thought he'd been followed, he would've ordered the eggs and mushrooms and eaten them with a fork to warn Arthur off when he passed by.

The raspberry filling was overly sweet in Micah's mouth, cloying. He should've ordered the cheese.

After a completely innocuous conversation with only a few codewords dropped in to indicate that Micah was on the cusp of a large operation, "a business venture of magnitude," and that intelligence support was requested, "venture capital financing," the two men wrapped up their discussion.

With that, Arthur picked up the briefcase closest to himself, shook Micah's hand, and made his way out of the café.

Micah pinned the micro-USB drive Arthur had passed to his palm with his thumb. He left his hands on the table for a minute just in case someone watched security camera footage later, even picking up the Danish to take a bite while the half-inch square was stuck to his palm. He was dang careful not to eat it, though.

Outside the café, a small liveaboard houseboat chugged into a slip in reverse, fountaining sea water onto the quay and frightening the pedestrians.

After a few minutes, Micah stood and patted his pants pocket for a few euros to leave on the table so he could drop the USB drive in his pocket.

He took his time sipping his coffee to watch for others who might be loitering, and then he picked up the briefcase Arthur had left to take back to Twist's yacht.

Back in his cabin, Micah opened the briefcase and

pulled out another USB drive, a larger one this time. *Novode-vichy Cemetery* was printed on the side of the thumb drive along with the logo he'd seen when Twist had been researching the Russian-owned company the day before.

Nice. If Micah was caught, the drive would look like he'd stolen something from Ostrovsky and the *Chekhovskaya* bratva, and there was still a chance they'd stick it in one of their computers and fulfill the mission. He chuckled as he tucked it in a drawer for the next day and took the briefcase to Twist.

In Twist's computer office, Micah and Twist examined the contents of the briefcase. Flying drones the size of bumblebees, large cellophane-backed stickers, and a bundle of three-inch-long wires with two small buttons on the ends.

Twist grinned. "Looks like you got it all. I'll call Blaze and Logan."

Micah bit his lip for a second before he said, "Just Blaze. Logan Bell might be a risk."

28

ENHANCED INTERROGATION TECHNIQUES

KYLIE

"So, what's the plan?" Kylie asked Micah when she returned to their cabin after doing her GED homework on the main deck for hours and hours until her brain was lost in a fog of Shakespeare and algebra.

Micah was working in their cabin on Twist's yacht, propped up on pillows in the bed with his laptop on his knees. He mumbled without looking up. "It's coming together."

A mild winter storm had rolled in before noon, and cool rain pattered on the roof and deck outside the expansive windows. When Kylie had been studying in the living room area, heavy clouds had hung in the sky from the mountains around the harbor to the horizon over the sea.

Call it a taunt, call it an opening, call it an ultimatum, but Kylie was calling Micah's bluff. He'd said that he trusted her, but did he?

She climbed on the bed and straddled his thighs, standing up on her knees. "But *what* is the plan?"

He looked up at her, startled. The golden light from the

lamp beside the bed caught the silver and green in his eyes. "It's coming together. Don't worry about it."

"I'm not worried, Micah. I trust that you can do this, too. I just want to know what I'm in for."

"You're not going to be there."

"The hell I'm not. This is *my* mother and *my* sister we're talking about. I need to be there so they'll cooperate. Otherwise, you're just more kidnappers to them."

Micah frowned and looked back to his screen quickly. "There is that."

"I don't know what that means, but I *will* be in the cars that go to the site tomorrow."

He frowned. "I'll consider it."

Oh, no. Kylie was going. Micah could *consider* until his ass turned blue, but she was going to be in those cars the next day. "You haven't even told me where we're going."

"We're not sure about the timeline or the exact target yet—"

It was four o'clock in the afternoon. "You'd better figure those out soon, rice cake, because this operation could theoretically start in twelve hours or less."

"More like eighteen hours, but I'm not comfortable divulging—"

Speaking of bulging, or it was at least close or whatever, Kylie's thighs around Micah's legs were having a physiological effect. She moved one leg, rubbing the outside of his thigh with her knee.

Kylie could see the vibration flow across Micah's skin like a wave on a lake.

Oh, she was going to get that information out of him one way or another.

Kylie grasped the top of Micah's laptop with her fingers,

plucked it out of his hands, and set it on the nightstand beside the bed, leaving nothing but her above him.

Micah said, "Hey, I was using that."

Kylie traced one fingernail over Micah's taut fly. "And if you tell me what I want to know, I'll be using *that.*"

"Kylie, this is ridiculous. I assure you, I'm not so easily manipulated."

She slid her fingernail over the straining fabric again and then circled his pants over his balls. This time, the shiver on his skin was like a rock thrown into a pond, the ripples spreading until they reached every one of his fingertips. "You sure you don't want to be manipulated like that?"

"I'm not going to tell you everything you want to know just because you're laying a honey trap."

Micah had no idea how good Kylie was at being a honey trap. "Come on. It'll be fun."

"Of that, I have no doubt, but playing games like that isn't—" But whatever he was going to say was cut off with a gasp.

While he'd been prattling on, Kylie had carefully unzipped his pants and dipped to suck his cock into her mouth.

Micah's fingers threaded into her hair, and he groaned.

When she looked up, he'd dropped his head back to rest on the bed's headboard, and his heel pushed against the bedspread on one side of her.

Kylie lifted her head and released him from her mouth with a pop. Violet veins protruded underneath his thin skin, and the engorged head was rosy.

Micah had grabbed handfuls of the comforters and was holding on with both fists, and he rolled his head to look at her through slitted eyes when she stopped.

The floor rocked under Kylie's feet from the storm

outside as she slid off the bed and shucked off her clothes, letting them fall on the thick rug around the king-size bed.

Micah was watching her intensely, his fists tightening on the wadded bedspread.

Naked, Kylie crawled onto the bed, the mattress bending under her knee. "Scoot down."

Micah's jaw bulged. "I beg your pardon?"

Kylie stared straight at him, feeling the showdown in her soul. "I said, scoot down. Lie flat on your back."

Micah's eyes seemed to be narrowed in anger, but he complied, inching his body down the bed until he laid flat.

Perfect.

Kylie crept until she stood on her knees across his pelvis, the zipper from his fly nipping the inside of her thigh. "Tell me where we're going tomorrow."

"It's going to take a lot more than that for me to—"

"*Fine.* Waterboarding, it is."

She walked her knees up his body, settled with her knees straddling his head, and then lowered herself onto his face.

Micah's hands slapped her hips, his fingertips digging into the soft skin of her ass. He held her down as his tongue explored the tender skin between her legs, and he sucked her clit.

Within seconds, Kylie dug her fingernails into the headboard as pleasure ran up her body and bowed her back.

Damn, this sexual interrogation method was backfiring.

With all her willpower, Kylie stood up on her knees despite Micah's best efforts. She asked, "Where is the operation tomorrow?"

"Warehouse over in France, north of here," he growled, and he pulled her hips back down so he could tongue her delicate membranes.

Her body was tightening, points and nerves becoming more sensitive and shivering.

Against every instinct screaming for Kylie to grind down on his mouth, she lifted one knee and teetered to the side.

Micah's hands waved in the empty air, and he wiped his face on his shirt sleeve as he rolled to sitting and reached for her.

Kylie held a hand up to stop him, keeping the other one clutching the headboard so she wouldn't fall over sideways. "Take off your clothes."

Micah bounded off the bed and peeled his clothes off his body, hopping as his trouser leg locked around one ankle, and he nearly ripped his pants getting his leg free.

"On the bed. Lay on your back," she panted.

Micah fell spreadeagle across the bed. The angry energy in his movements and his hands clawing at the bed linens betrayed his impulses.

"Don't move." Kylie lay on his chest, her legs molded around his hips as his erection nudged against her core. "Tell me what you know about the warehouse."

Micah grabbed handfuls of the blue quilt covering the bed and turned his fists to twist the fabric around his hands. The result didn't act as restraints so much as handles he could grip.

He spoke all at once. "I can't tell you how I know. We have pictures of people we think are your mother and sister."

Relief rushed into Kylie's body.

"*If* we're right. *If* it's them," he ground out, squeezing his eyes shut.

"Are they okay?"

"It looks like they're being held there. They appear to be in good health. At the very least, not injured, not restrained.

The mission is, first, reconnaissance. If they're there, rescue. *Come on.*"

Kylie eased back, pushing herself over him and taking him inside her. Her body was so sensitive from his mouth and tongue that she felt him slide all the way inside. The friction on her clit when she nestled down atop him nearly dropped her over the edge, and she breathed slowly, holding back.

Micah curled his fists like he was hanging on and arched his neck. "Damn, that's *hot.*"

She rocked on him, pushing herself back over him and then releasing him while Micah groaned under her.

Then, she stopped at the apex of a stroke, hovering just out of his tip's reach. "More details."

He said, "We've had drones flying inside the warehouse since yesterday afternoon. They're small. We haven't seen your mother or sister yet, but we're just seeing the tops of people's heads in the few areas we're watching. We haven't seen anyone struggling or being held prisoner. They're preparing an area for the painting."

Kylie flipped over and slid down over his cock, then sat up, reverse cowgirl-style.

Micah's tortured gasp was gratifying as hell.

She moved on him, riding him, and he bucked beneath her.

And she stopped again.

"And the plan tomorrow is what?"

"I go in to inspect the area for the painting. Blaze and Twist will be with me. We'll all be armed to the gills. I'll find some bullshit excuse to demand a thorough inspection of the whole warehouse before delivering the art. We already know the layout because Twist got a drone into the air conditioning ductwork. We mapped the air ducts, so we know where the walls are. If we find your family, we draw on the goombahs and take them with us. I called in a friend for help with the escape."

Kylie slid over his cock again, filling her, rubbing the sensitive parts inside her. "And I'm going with you tomorrow."

"Yes," Micah groaned. *"God, yes."*

She moved on him, grinding down, but Micah's hands clutched her hips and pushed her down on him. In seconds, she became a helpless thing he controlled.

Micah pumped her down on himself, bracing his legs and thrusting into her body. Ecstasy caught and blasted through her body, twisting and bending her backward. A cry tore from her throat and her body flopped bonelessly as he forced her down on him, taking her until he arched and grunted. One of his legs jittered as he released inside her.

His body collapsed under her, and Kylie held herself up with her hands braced on his legs, breathing hard.

Damn, she'd thought she was in charge, but he'd been playing with her.

But it had worked.

29

HOW TO CREATE AN OIL PAINTING
MICAH

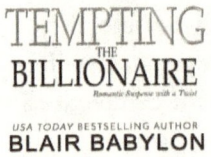

F irst, prepare the space.

Micah strolled through the empty Italian warehouse, watching the custodians sweep out the last dust after it had been cleared. The warehouse was just over the Italian border from France and, more importantly, within inches of the dimensions that the drones had determined the size of the Novodevichy Cemetery warehouse was.

Far above, steel girders interlaced and formed the rafters. The last of the rain storm pattered on the steel roof, but sunshine was breaking through the clouds and beaming sunset-tinted light through the westward windows.

The doors at the end opened. Tristan "Twist" King walked in, another man walking with him.

Micah broke off pacing the dimensions of the warehouse and hurried over. "Blaze, I appreciate you doing me that favor in Atlantic City. Did the girls leave the area safely?"

Blaze Robinson was the fourth of the Scholarship Mafia quartet from the Le Rosey boarding school. As indecently tall as the rest of them, Blaze was a Midwestern American like Twist, but dark-haired and dashing with a strong jaw and cheekbones reminiscent of generations of Scandinavian farmers. His pale, Nordic blue-fire eyes were another genetic remnant of his Viking ancestors who'd looked to the sea to find new lands to conquer and defend.

Twist and Blaze had earned their Le Rosey scholarships with pluck and academic excellence. Micah's scholarship, and, he suspected, Logan's as well, had been procured the old-fashioned way, with connections and money changing hands.

Blaze held out his hand as Micah approached. "I purchased a used SUV for the three women and a booster seat for the toddler. It's registered in my name, and I watched them drive out of that wretched apartment and turn for the freeway. They're fine. I told them to buy prepaid phones to contact you and Kylie once they're settled. They assured me they would, but it might take a while."

"I can't express how much I appreciate it. Kylie was beside herself. She's the most loyal person I know, and not going back there to help them was about to tear her apart."

Blaze gestured to the empty warehouse. His voice had a bit more gravel to it than the other two, as if there was hard use in its past. "And this is your next project. It's interesting you called for backup. Usually, you're on the other end of the phone when one of us calls."

Micah shrugged. "It's just happened that way. It's good to see you."

Blaze's rueful smile was embarrassed. "It's good to see you, too." He barreled into Micah for a tight hug and then released him, staring up at the warehouse windows. "So this is it, the staging area for the operation."

"Indeed," Micah said.

Start over.

First, prepare the space.

When creating a work of art using oil paints, the first step is to prepare the supplies and the space, making sure the paints, oils, solvents, brushes, canvases, and the easel are ready for the work.

The warehouse was rented for a week, and Micah had diagrams and masking tape.

He handed a large roll of blue tape to Blaze, who teased the end away from the underlying layers and tabbed it, so it was ready to use.

Second, prepare the blank canvas by sealing it with primer.

The floor had been swept, but Micah directed the custodians hired for the day to run wide mops over the expanse to ensure the tape would stick before they were dismissed.

Ready.

Then, sketch the blocks of your image, making sure the proportions and values of your paint are correct.

Micah used his phone to shoot precise measurements, and he, Blaze, and Twist sketched lines with tape on the cement floor to represent the walls of the Novodevichy Cemetery warehouse in France.

The result was a rabbit warren of rooms. Some were larger for storage, but some had been converted into office space or just smaller spaces meant to confuse authorities looking for something in particular.

Fourth, begin to add color.

Using thinned paint, block in the major shapes of the image with their colors and the blank spaces in neutral gray. Use black rarely and sparingly, but never white.

Blaze, Twist, and Micah walked through their entrance

to the warehouse and traced the paths where they would most likely be led.

Their route would be direct but innocuous. If Anatoly Ostrovsky, or the *Chekhovskaya* bratva in particular, didn't want Micah and the other two to see something, they would be led around it.

They should recognize what spaces they were being led around.

The three men practiced when to turn their heads to glance inside other rooms, how a few steps down another corridor before their hypothetical guide noticed their mistake might allow a glimpse into places they weren't supposed to see.

Between the three of them and a few bits of misdirection, they figured they could view over half the spaces in the warehouse instead of the less than twenty percent they might have seen without careful planning.

Next, build colors and shapes with more concentrated paint.

The three men sat on chairs in the middle of the cement-floored expanse, memorizing the taped layout around them. They practiced ruses, banter, and personas that they might use while they were inside the Novodevichy Cemetery warehouse.

Finally, add details and smaller blocks without breaking up the large blocks of color in the initial outline.

As they hashed out more details, some ideas were discarded, like calling in certain friends of theirs who owned a personal military because then they'd have to admit that Micah had stolen invaluable art from a Mafia kingpin.

Others were discussed in more detail and length.

After hours of walk-throughs and brainstorming, Blaze

looked around the warehouse lit by the fluorescent tube lights in the ceiling and the darkness outside the windows. "The cars are leaving at nine tomorrow morning?"

"Nine-fifteen," Micah said. "Ten o'clock arrival."

Twist asked, "And it's going to be just us three?"

Micah nodded. "Yep. Just us."

30

HER CHANCE

KYLIE

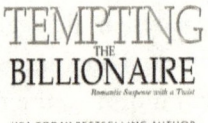

TEMPTING
THE
BILLIONAIRE
Romantic Suspense with a Twist

USA TODAY BESTSELLING AUTHOR
BLAIR BABYLON

K ylie was told that the cars going to the Novodevichy Cemetery's warehouse would be leaving at two in the afternoon.

Two cars had been rented and would be dropped off at the yacht club's pickup zone an hour before the anticipated departure time.

Micah set his phone's alarm for six, Kylie noted.

That was an early wake-up time for a two o'clock meeting.

But she didn't call him on it. She didn't need to.

He was up, showered, and out of their cabin by six-thirty, taking the stairs two at a time to meet the other two guys on the main deck above.

Right.

Kylie was ready at seven in the morning, black-clad like a theater technician to her jawline, fingertips, and toes. She kept away from the three guys but watched out the wide window of their cabin. She fished a small backpack from under the bed where they'd been stashing extra stuff and dumped a few bottles of water and snacks inside.

Come down for breakfast, Micah texted.

I'm sleeping in, she wrote back. *After all, the cars don't leave for hours.*

That's true, he texted back.

No, it wasn't.

Kylie listened to the thumps, creaks, and lapping waves as the yacht rolled in the calm marina waters, and she watched the floating wooden sidewalk and cement quay that led to the shore through the cabin's wide window.

At eight o'clock that morning, the three guys thundered down the spiral staircase on the stern end of the yacht and, as Kylie watched from a cracked door in the hallway, closeted themselves in Twist's windowless computer room and shut the door.

That was her chance.

31

THE GIGGLING LUMP

MICAH

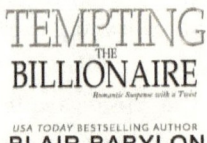

Micah opened the liftgate of the black SUV and dumped the duffel bag inside, metal clanking as the hatch descended.

As he walked around to the driver's side and stepped in, a peek in the backseat afforded him a glimpse of a wadded-up quilt in the back seat that looked remarkably like the cream underside of the comforter in his cabin on Twist's yacht.

Micah paused as he sat in the driver's seat, his finger poised above the start button on the dash, contemplating.

The sun was still low in the sky on that late fall morning, just cresting the mountaintops and beaming sunlight on the earth-hued high-rises packed together on the mountainsides above the harbor.

In the rearview mirror, Twist and Blaze were stepping into the second SUV they'd rented, both of them looking somber.

Micah tapped the vehicle's start button and pulled away from the Quai Louis II road in front of the yacht club, spinning the steering wheel in a sharp U-turn to merge into traffic and speed into the maw of one of Monaco's traffic tunnels.

The yacht club had been built in an area of Monaco named for Prince Louis II, the wartime Prince of Monaco who sympathized too much with the Vichy French government because an old friend of his from the French Foreign Legion was running it. While Monaco protected most of its small Jewish population by issuing them official false identification papers during World War II, about a third of them were rounded up by the Monegasque police on the insistence of the Vichy government, sent to the camps, and died.

The heir to the throne, who became Prince Rainier III and Grace Kelly's husband, bitterly fought his grandfather Prince Louis II, trying to protect Monaco's Jewish citizens more and bring Monaco into the war on the Allies' side.

Or so Micah had been told while drinking late at night in high school with Rainier III's grandson, who had not been the heir to the throne and put in his lowly place his whole life, but who'd ended up inheriting the principality and the power, nevertheless.

Still, the streets were named after Louis II. Maybe Max would change them now that he ruled the place.

Inside the Tunnel Louis II, square lights lined the ceilings and walls and glowed on the reflective tile, brightening the narrow roadway inside. Micah steered the SUV through the curves. Getting pulled over would derail the operation and probably send him to jail.

Ten minutes after he emerged from the tunnel and had been dodging the tourist-rented Bugattis and Lamborghinis, Micah announced, "I'll bet if I tickled that lump in the backseat, it would giggle."

As he'd expected, Kylie struggled to fight her way out from under the comforter, and she clambered between the bucket seats in front to throw herself into the passenger seat. "You were going to leave without me."

"I now see the futility of that."

He did. He should have either just invited her to come along or tied her to the bed.

But then *he* probably would've been late.

Kylie strapped her seatbelt on. She was wearing some kind of ninja costume that instantly had him thinking of seductresses who sneaked into bedrooms and ravaged unsuspecting men like himself.

Micah wore a designer Armani suit, as befitted an art dealer selling an enormously valuable piece of art. "You're not dressed to come in with us."

"Oh, yes, I am coming in with you. I'm going to rescue my sister and my mom."

Micah shook his head, though he didn't look away from the congested streets of Monaco while driving. "Take my phone. The most recent photo is a schematic of the likely configuration inside the warehouse. Memorize it."

Kylie eyed him as if he might snatch the phone back from her, but he unlocked it with a quick flick of his watch so she could see the map.

While she examined it, he told her the general outline of the plan, at least the part that he had told Twist and Blaze. "We'll be conducting surveillance as we are led through to inspect the accommodations for the painting. If we find where your mother or sister are being held, we will make an impromptu decision as to whether we will immediately try for an extraction or wait until nightfall. If we don't find them, we will have reduced the area that we need to search by at least half for when we break in tonight."

"So, there's no way to know whether they are there or not."

"We haven't seen anyone struggling or restrained even though we've had surveillance drones in the warehouse or almost twenty-four hours. It's possible they aren't there, despite our best intelligence."

"But we're going to look, right?"

"Yes, *cara mia,* we're going to look."

Kylie was quiet, her dark eyebrows furrowed, as she studied the map, turning his phone and expanding the schematic with reverse pinches to see the details.

"There's more, and there is something you can do for us."

"Yeah?"

"Under your seat, there's an iPad." While she bent over double to feel around, Micah told her, "We've had seven bumblebee-sized drones in the warehouse for the last twenty-four hours."

Kylie gasped, *"Have you seen my mom or my sister?"*

"No, we haven't. We haven't seen anyone who might be a prisoner or restrained, and we've only been able to see the tops of people's heads for the most part. It doesn't mean they're not there."

She sighed, a whoosh of air that cramped Micah's chest.

He said, "You can watch the feeds for us. If anything looks wrong, text me. It'll buzz my watch."

"I will," she said, studying both the iPad and his phone and dragging the pictures around to correlate the images.

"And there's one more surveillance drone." Micah patted his left pec. "It's in my pocket square. You'll see everything I do."

Kylie nodded.

"You have an important job," he told her.

She nodded again. "Yeah, okay."

"But you have to promise me you won't leave the car."

She snapped her head around and stared at him. *"You must be joking,"* she snarled.

"No, seriously. You're our tech support. You have to stay in the car."

"Dude, *no way.*"

"And if we get caught, you need to take this SUV and leave."

"I would *never* abandon you like that."

"I mean it. Here's the fob." He slapped it into her outstretched hand. "There's a second SUV. If we get out, we'll ride in that one. But I won't go if you're not safe, so I *need* you to be *safe.*"

"Okay, okay. I get it. I'll make sure I'm safe."

Micah reached into his suit jacket, removing a handgun from a holster on his hip, and handed it to her butt-first. "You can shoot one of these things, right?"

"No!" Kylie held it gingerly with two fingers. "What the hell do I look like, a barbarian?"

"They don't teach New Jersey Mafia princesses to shoot guns?"

"I sure as hell wasn't a *princess,* and I thought these things were illegal in Europe."

"Twist has a small militia's worth of weapons hidden in his computer office behind the bank of monitors. When I asked why, he glared at me and said something like, 'Because I can afford them.'"

She held it back out to him. "You should take it."

"I have another one. I'll give you the holster when we find someplace to pull over."

"Yeah, okay." She inserted the pistol gingerly into a shelf in the SUV's dash, the muzzle pointed away from both of them. At least she had some common sense about it.

Kylie asked him, "Is that all of the plan? Look around and then maybe get them out if you see them?"

"Yeah. That's all we've got," Micah lied.

He paused.

Lying about his other training, his reason for existing, was as easy as breathing, which is what he'd been trained to do. He didn't even *think* about it unless he was standing in Arthur Finch-Hatten's deer park or in the middle of an operation.

Micah gripped the steering wheel more tightly.

A cartoon line on the car's navigation screen and a sudden decrease in housing density were the only signs they'd crossed the invisible international border to France. French houses came with fewer vertical stories, larger gardens, and income tax.

The SUV's tires ground on the rougher road as Micah followed the GPS toward the more dilapidated part of the countryside.

The GPS counted down the time, indicating they would reach their destination in ten minutes.

As he watched the road, Micah said aloud, "I'm working with Interpol and MI-6 to destroy international crime syndicates. Grande's and Genevese's LCN organizations were first. That's why I started the Mafia war, so they'd destroy each other. Next are the Sokolovs and Butorin bratva families. After that, I've got another target."

Kylie turned and stared at him. *"What the hell, Micah?"*

"The world will be better off without them. I know it's whack-a-mole, that others will arise to take their places, but the human trafficking and imprisonment and graft and theft and blackmail and *murder have to stop."*

Her dark eyes flashed with anger. "You should have told me."

"Arthur Finch-Hatten is my handler. He's MI-6, but he works with Interpol, too. He recruited me when I was a senior in high school because he knew who I was, or who I used to be. I didn't even know that he knew until recently."

From the corner of his eye, he could see Kylie glaring at him, but he was watching the rough-paved road and micromanaging the car's path to avoid potholes.

She snarked at him, "Oh, and I *don't* know who you are?"

The swirling storm of words blew out of him. "Vincent Genovese murdered my whole family when I was ten, but he missed me. My father's friends hid me for a few weeks until they could arrange for a scholarship to Le Rosey to get me out of the country. They gave me a new name. It was easier back then. You could get a dead baby's birth certificate from the county office and become them. Now, everything's computerized."

She was still glaring at him like she was trying to laser the top of his head off. "What's your real name?"

"Marcu Argento."

She flopped in the passenger seat. "Argento means silver in Italian, so that's where you got *Shine.*"

"Just luck, or they might have picked one close so I wouldn't forget it because I was ten."

"So, your plan is to *destroy* the bratva that owns the warehouse?"

"My primary plan is to rescue your mother and sister if they're there. Otherwise, I wouldn't have involved Twist and Blaze. But yes, I have a thumb drive that I'm going to insert into any computer I can access. It'll download malware from the internet that will clone every hard drive in the network and upload them to Interpol's databases."

"That's what you did to Salvatore Grande!"

"His firewalls were too good for this type of malware.

Arthur had already probed them. I just cloned his computer onto the thumb drive, but it gave us the information so we knew where to look for Rachele and your mother."

"Well, goddamn," Kylie said. "You're a narc."

"I prefer spy."

"Whatever."

And now for the moment of truth. He asked, "Are we still doing this?"

"Hell, yeah. These assholes kidnapped my mother and sister. Let's burn their whole organization to the ground."

Micah didn't take his eyes off the road, but he reached over and took her hand. "No, I meant, are we still doing *this*."

She squeezed his hand. "Always."

32

THE WAREHOUSE
MICAH

M icah parked the SUV next to a winter-bare hedge of sticks on the far side of the parking lot from the warehouse rented by the Novode-vichy Cemetery organization. Kylie was sitting on the back seat floor with the comforter tented over her position with the iPad and her phone.

After the recent rainstorm, a chill had swept through the region, cooling even the temperate South of France to a wintry nip.

The second rented SUV parked next to his.

Blaze glanced through the windows between them with no expression on his face, just a solid, square jaw that was neither slack nor clenched, perhaps with a slight narrowing of his frost-blue eyes.

At precisely two minutes before ten o'clock, Micah buttoned his suit jacket over his stomach and walked toward the low building without a backward glance.

Pale gravel crunched under his shoes, but he kept his head up as if he were mildly interested in nothing.

Blaze and Twist followed Micah toward the door, their

footsteps scratching on the rocky ground like talons on cement.

Micah raised his fist to knock at the solid-steel door, but the door was already swinging open. Warmer air rolled out, engulfing Micah's face and carrying the dusty foulness of long-stored plastic breaking down into solvents and the decay of dead rodents. The speed that the stench overwhelmed the parking lot's sunshine-baked earth was alarming.

Anatoly Ostrovsky stood inside, beckoning Micah and the others to enter. "Is good to see you. I am pleased to show you our accommodations for the art."

Micah stepped in, shook Ostrovsky's rough hand, and then gestured at Twist and Blaze. "Good to see you again, Anatoly. These are my friends, John and Tom."

Why advertise, indeed.

After handshakes all around, Anatoly led the three of them through the warehouse, trailed by two unintroduced rough-hewn blocks of men who twitched at the buzz of a wasp up by the ceiling.

First corridor, five steps, turn head to the left.

Shrink-wrapped pallets filled the metal shelves of the sectioned-off area. A forklift whined as it drove down the broad aisle, looking for something to stick its prongs in and lift.

As planned, the three of them alternated peering between each stack of shelves or into corridors they passed so that two faces were always facing forward, certainly not surveilling, and one person was looking for Kylie's family or some indication someone was being held prisoner.

Micah was also looking for unsecured computers.

Six steps, turn head to the right.

A shorter corridor than the one on the left, stacked

shelves filled with plastic-mummified boxes on pallets, and a sheetrock wall where one shouldn't be.

Micah coughed lightly and then sniffed, code for *to the left, suspicious.*

A few seconds later, Twist sneezed. *Confirmation. Suspicious thing to the left.*

They continued looking as they were led halfway into the warehouse and then turned to the right.

Blaze was looking up as if distracted by the utilitarian tube lighting above their heads and got ten feet farther down the central corridor before the goons behind them returned him, apologizing for his absentmindedness, to the herd.

When Micah glanced back at him, Blaze scratched his cheek. *Saw nothing.*

Micah's watch buzzed on his left wrist. He checked it with a brief glance.

Car. 3 ppl. Going inside.

The lack of any other information told him that it was *not* three armed bodyguards sprinting inside with purpose, nor was it two prison guards dragging a prisoner out of the car.

Their little lookout was doing her job from the car, where she was hopefully safe. *Excellent.*

Anatoly Ostrovsky led the group, nattering on about his commitment to art conservation. Micah made sure to grunt encouraging sounds every now and then. Twist and Blaze walked in silence, watching.

Finally, they reached a locked door in a wall of hastily nailed-together drywall.

Ostrovsky made a big show of taking out his keys to unlock it. Micah paid ostentatious attention to Anatoly Ostrovsky while listening as carefully as possible to every scratch and wheeze of the air conditioning and people moving within the warehouse now that they'd stopped walking.

Ostrovsky put on a proper dog-and-pony show inside the vault room for Micah and his guys, extolling the climate control and security systems in the room and the warehouse.

Blaze and Twist examined the walls, nodding sagely, during the lecture.

Micah listened until Ostrovsky ran out of words and then said, "Show me more about your warehouse's security system."

After that, they got the grand tour, walking the perimeter of the building inside and out. Micah and the guys found two more locations of interest within the building and memorized the numbers Ostrovsky typed into the keypads.

Breaking in that night was going to be a cinch.

When they walked back inside the warehouse to an office area cross-hatched with cubicles, Anatoly Ostrovsky asked Micah, "So, everything is to your liking?"

Micah nodded and smiled. "You have an excellent set-up here, Anatoly. We can arrange payment and delivery of the painting as soon as possible."

Ostrovsky grinned like a kid behind a pile of birthday presents. "Are you going to tell me what it is now?"

Micah leaned toward him, a prim smile curving his lips. "*The Annunciation* by Lorenzo di Credi."

Ostrovsky's grin stretched his face into a mass of pointy wrinkles. "Di Credi? And a religious subject? It is very nice. I am very happy with arrangement."

"As am I, Anatoly." Micah stuck out his hand to shake on it.

Out of the corner of his eye, Micah caught Twist and Blaze rolling their eyes and resuming their inspection of the warehouse with that night's infiltration in mind.

Micah was still shaking hands with Anatoly when more footsteps rounded a corner. The more brittle taps of a woman's footwear on the industrial tile beneath their feet registered before he turned around.

Ostrovsky looked at the woman behind Micah and grinned harder, releasing his hand. "Micah Shine, may I present my associate, Ms. Sofia Maximovna Melnik. She is especially interested in having Old Master painting."

Beside him, Twist and Blaze looked at the new arrival, smiling and nodding in greeting.

Micah turned, careful to keep his face as blank as a primed canvas, even though he knew what he would see.

Melnik meant *miller* in Russian, as in someone who operates a mill and grinds grain into flour.

Miller.

Kylie Miller hadn't picked her surname by accident or because it was similar to Merlino. It was the Anglicization of her mother's maiden name.

Sofia Melnik looked precisely like the composite Micah had seen for a week with traces of her daughter around her straight nose and soft mouth, but he never would have imagined the bright blond hair Sofia had been hiding under all those scarves.

Too late, he slapped his hand over the bumblebee-sized drone hiding the pocket square of his suit jacket.

His watch buzzed again and again.

33

RACHELE

KYLIE

K ylie was sitting in the SUV holding the iPad at arm's length, her heartbeat pounding in her temples.

She had heard the Russian guy Anatoly Ostrovsky say *her mother's name*, Sofia Melnik.

He'd even known her mother's middle name was Maximovna.

When Micah had turned around and his video feed had swung with him, panning over the office space within the warehouse, Kylie had *seen* her mother's neck and face.

Like her life flashing before her eyes, images of her mother in Kylie's life crashed around her like breaking dishes.

Her mother sitting on the beach with Kylie and Rachele, laughing at them as they played in the waves while smoking a cigarette.

Kylie tapped the microphone icon on her phone's screen to dictate a text to Micah. "You found her. *You found her.*"

Her mother speaking another language into the phone, a

language Kylie and Rachele weren't allowed to learn because they had to learn Italian and Sicilian.

She dictated into the phone, "You found my mom. *That's my mom.*"

Her mother sending Kylie off to school that morning after a stupid fight about whether the shirt Kylie was wearing was too tight, waving but not looking as Kylie had left their small house.

She dictated, "Tell her I'm here. Tell her *I'm coming.*"

Her mother was standing *right there* with Micah in that warehouse, her blond hair loose and curling around her shoulders, not at all like the tight ballet buns Kylie remembered from four years before.

Her mother was standing *right there,* being introduced by her maiden name as if her life of being Joseph Merlino's wife and Kylie's mother had never happened.

Time stuttered sideways.

Her mother was standing *right there* like she hadn't left her underaged teenage daughter alone in Atlantic City.

Kylie begged, "Tell her not to leave. *Tell her I'm coming.*"

The iPad was falling out of Kylie's hands and her hands were scrabbling toward the SUV's door and she was stumbling across the gravel parking lot, yanking open the door, and falling inside and crying as she ran, "Mom! *Mom!*"

Inside the warehouse, the shelves all looked the same. Kylie darted to the left and then the right, trying to find the office.

A door in the long wall looked like it might have an office behind it, so Kylie sprinted over and yanked it open. *"Mom?"*

Inside was not the multi-person rabbit warren of cubicles Kylie had seen on Micah's video feed.

Instead, it was a single office with a manager's desk in the middle and a smaller desk against the wall.

A teenage girl with light brown hair who was sitting at the desk twisted herself around as Kylie opened the door.

School books were stacked messily on the desk, their titles in French.

The girl looked startled, but her hazel eyes widened. *"Chiarina?"*

Shock slapped Kylie. *"Rachele?"*

And then Rachele vaulted at Kylie, grabbing her around the neck and sobbing and kissing her face. "We thought you were *dead*. Mom said that they had *killed* you, the same as Daddy. *Chiarina*, I can't believe you're *okay*. It's like seeing a ghost. It's like if Daddy walked in. Where did you go? *How did you survive?*"

Kylie grabbed Rachele, hugging the stuffing out of her and holding on because she couldn't believe she'd found her sister. "I don't know what you're talking about. I came home from school, and you and Mom were *gone*. I've been looking for you ever since."

Rachele leaned back but didn't let go of Kylie. "Mom picked me up from school at lunchtime. Mom had our suitcases. We went to the airport and waited for you, but you never came. She said we had to go. We got on a plane that afternoon and went and stayed with Mom's relatives in Moscow, and then she told me when we got there that you had died. Did you know she was going to *Russia* all those times she visited her mother?"

Kylie shook her head. "She told me she was going to Indiana."

"It was never Indiana. Her mother lives in Moscow. We were there for a few months before we came here."

Regret and loss pummeled Kylie. "My high school must not have given me the message. The front desk was shit for things like that. *I would have come.* I would have come *with you*. I've lived in Atlantic City alone all these years."

Rachele's eyes squeezed closed, and her arms gripped Kylie's neck. "You live in Atlantic City? Like, you have an apartment or something?"

"It's a slum. I mean, it's really awful," Kylie admitted.

Rachele's crying turned to sobbing. "Take me with you. Let's go someplace else, *anyplace else*. Like California or something. *Get me out of here before Mom finds us.*"

34

SOFIA MAXIMOVNA MELNIK

MICAH

Micah stared at Kylie's mother and agreed that Sicilian genes were strong and Kylie *must* take after her father.

Sofia Maximovna Melnik had a square face, broad cheekbones and jaw, and bleached-out blue eyes to match her platinum-blond hair.

The cold disgust in Sofia's stare was disturbing and so different from her daughter. Kylie had never squinted with the corners of her eyes or pressed her teeth in a snarl like that, not even when she was mad as hell.

Mafia dons and capos didn't glare at anyone like that, either. Unless they were about to whack someone and sometimes even then, they were unflaggingly polite. Everyone was shocked that such a nice guy could order murders and extort entire neighborhoods.

But Sofia Maximovna Melnik? Micah would believe anything of a person with that snake-eyed glare.

This woman clearly didn't need rescuing.

Maybe, and Micah prayed to all the saints but especially St. Paul, the saint whose image was burned when Mafia associates became made men, *maybe* Kylie Miller had listened when he'd told her to stay the hell in the SUV where it was *safe.*

He grinned and held out his hand to shake, making sure his British accent was firmly in place. "Charmed, I'm sure."

"Yes, I'm sure," she said, shaking his hand with her cold hand and then dropping it.

"Anatoly Ostrovsky has done such an excellent job in creating a properly climate-controlled space for the art," Micah told her. "It's been a pleasure to work with him."

"Yes, Anatoly is pleasure to work with," Sofia said offhandedly, gazing back into the tube-lit office space. "It's been quite an experience."

Micah asked her, "Does your organization often wish to acquire or validate art?"

"Well, as things come our way, sometimes. We are not specialist organization like some. We are more flexible."

Micah asked her more general questions about her ambitions for her organization, nothing that could be considered prying but definitely things to get her talking about herself and her network. People love to talk about themselves and their work.

Time had passed, *minutes,* and Micah's watch had ceased buzzing.

Please, dear Madonna and St. Paul, please let Kylie have stayed in the car.

Sofia turned to Anatoly Ostrovsky and asked, "What did he say painting is?"

Anatoly Ostrovsky beamed at Sofia as if he were trying very hard for approval that would never happen. "*Annunciation* by Lorenzo di Credi."

Sofia swiveled back to Micah. "Which one? Di Credi painted *Annunciation* at least three times. Maybe more."

Micah grinned. As an art history major, he could debate fifteenth-century Italian paintings all day long. "It's his final one from circa 1503, where the Virgin Mary is wearing a blue robe and an Italianate garden is visible through architectural arches behind her."

"Right, one where she is so very blond, considering she supposed to be Jew." Sofia thought for a moment, looking up and to the left. Her jaw did not unclench. "So, it's forgery."

Micah lazily raised one eyebrow, not taking offense but in scorn. "It's been authenticated by the most modern technological means, by radioisotope dating as well as identifying components in the paint to be those used by di Credi in other masterworks, as well as image analysis to match it to prior images of the work. It's definitely *not* a forgery."

She didn't blink. "But *Annunciation* by Lorenzo di Credi was stolen from the *Musée des Beaux-Arts de Lyon* in France by Nazis during World War II."

"And it was never recovered. It's been in private collections ever since."

"Well, yes," Sofia said, leaning toward him. "It's been in Salvatore Grande's 'private collection,' and I use term very loosely, for last six years. I've regarded it every time I've sat in his office, staring at vapid angel with rainbow wings and surprised stupid girl who doesn't know where babies come from."

It wasn't an altogether wrong description of the painting. "That's the one."

Her eyes narrowed. "How did you get it from Salvatore? He didn't say he's selling it."

"The sale was not advertised to the general public. It's a private transaction for personal reasons beyond the excruciatingly obvious one that it was stolen from its rightful owner, the country of France, from a museum, *by the Nazis,*" Micah told her, leaning in as if divulging a secret. "France would *strenuously object* to any public sale and would reclaim it without compensation."

Blaze frowned as if Micah wasn't supposed to give that away. Micah's guys always had his back, even when uptight Blaze would rather not be lying.

Sofia nodded and said to Anatoly, "Salvatore Grande has gone to the mattresses with New York Genovese syndicate. They are hemorrhaging money. This must be why he is selling it."

To go to the mattresses, that old Mafia term for an internecine war between factions, was black humor for when many made men would lie down and not stand up again. The mafia slang must have traveled all the way to Europe.

Or Joseph Merlino might have said it around Sofia before he was murdered for being a rat.

Maybe Kylie had been a little girl in the room when he'd said it.

Micah said, "I'm not at liberty to discuss Mr. Grande's rationale for selling the work, but he is very sensitive about any discussion of it."

"Of course he is."

"Shine Industries prides itself on our discretion."

"Salvatore would work with a person like that."

"We're working very closely with Mr. Grande. Indeed, our business here is concluded, so we should be on our way." He gestured toward the door leading to the warehouse and out. "John and Tom, shall we?"

Twist and Blaze were a fraction of a second slow to respond, but it wasn't too noticeable.

Before Micah and his crew could reach the door leading to the warehouse, it swung open.

Kylie, still dressed in ninja-wear, and another, younger girl who could only have been her sister, Rachele, were propelled into the office by the two rough-hewn men who'd been following Micah, Blaze, and Twist around the warehouse earlier.

Kylie and Rachele were struggling to get away but could not so much as jiggle the men holding them.

Sofia gasped. *"Chiarina?"*

The wood block of a man on the left said, "We found this chick wandering around with Rachele. We took the guard off Rachele's door while these three were in the warehouse," pointing to Micah and the guys, "so they wouldn't be suspicious."

That had somewhat worked, Micah had to admit. "I say, what's this, now?"

No one was looking at him.

Perfect.

He sidled around a desk, looking at the computer on it.

Someone had left it running, and the screen glowed blue.

Kylie yelled at her mother, "Yeah, it's me. Rachele told me what you were going to *do with her.* How could you do that? *She's only fourteen years old!"*

Sofia said, "Anatoly, all of you, *get out.* I need this room."

Anatoly Ostrovsky and the few office workers *ran* for the door and exited.

"You shouldn't be here," Sofia said to Kylie, horror filling her pale eyes. "You are supposed to be in Atlantic City, working for Salvatore Grande."

"You told Rachele *I was dead.* Why did you *do* that?" Kylie yelled back at her.

Micah tapped the computer keyboard's space bar. It opened to the desktop, a few icons and files littering the screen.

Sofia Melnik shrugged. "It was easier than explaining why you weren't with us. Rachele was ten. She wouldn't have understood."

"My school didn't give me the message that you were leaving. I would have come. Why did you leave without me?"

Sofia tilted her head, the fluorescent lights bouncing off her shining hair. "There was no message."

"But Rachele said that you sent a message to meet you at the airport or to come home, and when I didn't show up, you said that I must be dead."

"You were for Salvatore Grande. I had to tell her something why you weren't going with us."

"Instead, you told her that I *died?*"

"What, she was fine."

"Why the hell did you *leave me?*" Kylie shouted at her mother. "I was *sixteen* when you *abandoned* me!"

Micah stood solidly, watching the family melodrama, while he fished in his trouser pocket for Arthur Finch-Hatten's USB drive.

Sofia turned one hand over, palm up, and her sneer was horrifying. "That was our price to leave. Salvatore Grande said you would work for him running cons or else he would take you for his wife."

Kylie shook her head. "No. *No way.* Besides, he's been married to Mrs. Grande for, like, forty years."

Sofia shrugged again. "She fall down stairs or something. No one would ask questions."

"Are you kidding me? And what you were going to do to Rachele is *worse.* She's only *fourteen!"*

"We were going to wait a while. Even Italian priests won't marry a girl until she's sixteen. It is just betrothal ceremony."

Micah's fingertips touched the thumb drive in his pocket, and he grabbed it.

"Mom! That's just gross! How can you do that to your *daughter?* Why did you do that to *me?"*

"It's not that big of deal, happens all the time. I don't know why you two are so upset about it. I was sixteen when I came to America to be with your father."

"You told us you met him in *Paris,"* Kylie accused her.

"Yeah, well, what we told you. *Chekhovskaya* bratva wanted to make connections with Nicky Scarfo, who was head of Philly section at that time, so they sent me as bride for one of his capos. Nicky Scarfo was before Salvatore Grande," Sofia said like she was lecturing on the history of the mob in Philadelphia.

Micah glanced at the computer on the desk, peeked at the USB drive to make sure he was holding the damn thing the right way because he didn't want to take two or three tries at it, and jabbed the thumb drive in the USB slot.

Kylie yelled at her mother, "That's *barbaric!"*

"No, it's business. My father was important in *Chekhovskaya* bratva at the time, and I was his daughter to do with what he wanted. Now I am important in *Chekhovskaya* bratva, and you are my daughters and will do what I tell you."

"You have internalized the patriarchy of the misogynistic Russian mafia, *Mom!"*

Micah smiled. *Atta girl.*

Sofia's voice dropped to a menacing snarl. "You will do what I say, Chiarina."

"It's *Kylie!* My name is *Kylie Miller!"*

The thumb drive whirred.

The computer growled.

The screen flickered but remained steady on the desktop, showing a few folders and the trash can.

Sofia said, "Kylie is stupid baby-name. You will call yourself Chiarina, like adult. You will stop fighting and spend night in Rachele's room. Tomorrow, I send you both to Philadelphia. Salvatore Grande can decide what to do with you, and you better not make fuss on plane, either. You are spoiled American girls. I should have treated you like real Russian mother."

Micah's watch flashed a blank screen of dark green.

Success!

He strolled away from the computer, calmly walking around the edge of the desk. "I'm leaving tonight on a private plane to the States. I can drop them off with Salvatore Grande in Philadelphia. It would be more secure than a commercial flight."

Kylie looked up at him from where she and Rachele were being restrained by Sofia's two goons and screamed, *"No! God, no!"*

She flailed, finally wrenching her arm away from Sofia's henchman and grabbing Rachele, trying to shield her.

Sofia glanced at Micah and back at her daughters. "You know him?"

"That's *Marcu Argento*," Kylie said, sobbing and holding onto Rachele even though the guy was trying to grab her arm again. "He's Salvatore's *worst* enforcer and right-hand man. He's *evil*. No one knows how many people he's killed. Even the police chief of Philadelphia shits his pants when *Marcu Argento* pays him a visit. *Please,* Mom, *no*. We'll be *good*. We'll get on a regular plane and fly there. *We won't make any trouble.*"

Like goddamn clockwork, Kylie fell right into Micah's plan.

Sofia turned to him. "Seems like you are more than just art dealer."

Micah shrugged and looked off into the office space. He let his New York accent bleed through the British one. "Yeah, *thank* you. *Thank* you."

Just like the La Cosa Nostra guys.

"You don't look Sicilian," she told him.

Micah chuckled. "I get that a lot. My mother was Norwegian."

"Ah, yes. Rachele takes after me, but my former husband's Sicilian genes are strong in Chiarina. That was about the only thing that was strong in him. I don't know how he got to be capo. I finally got tired of him and told Salvatore he had ratted him out." Sofia turned back to the girls. Kylie was gaping at her, her legs shaking. "Benny, get their things. You girls will fly with Marcu Argento back to Salvatore Grande."

Kylie let out an impressive wail that would have broken Micah's heart if he didn't know this was the best con she'd ever pulled.

He said, "John, Tom, get the girls. We'll take 'em with us."

Blaze and Twist walked over to Kylie and Rachele and took them off the cubic guys' hands.

Kylie renewed her struggles, and Blaze looked up at Micah. He pinned her hands behind her back and whispered something to her, and she sobbed, wiping her face on her shoulder.

Sofia said, "You aren't going to touch them, right? Rachele needs to be virgin for her marriage. Italians are traditional that way. I assume Chiarina is ruined."

Micah barely threw them a glance. "Too young. I like my women with some experience." He looked Sofia up and down quickly and then smiled at her.

She looked surprised and flirted back with him. "I didn't know that."

He stepped toward her, half a smile on his face, and kept his New York accent in place. "Look, I'm going to be back in Europe in a few weeks. Why don't I call you up, see if we can get together for a drink or something."

"Um, all right."

Sofia Maximovna Melnik was flustered.

And that meant she was distracted.

Kylie's fight to free herself became more enraged than terrified.

Sofia tapped her number into Micah's phone and handed it back to him.

"Yeah," he said. "I'll see you in a few weeks."

"Yes, I suppose so, if it works out. I'll call Salvatore and tell him you are bringing both Chiarina and Rachele to him tonight."

"Don't trouble yourself," Micah said as he walked over to his guys, Kylie, and Rachele. "I was going to call him from the car to tell him the deal for the di Credi is done. The painting will be delivered tonight, by the way. You should make sure Anatoly Ostrovsky is ready to receive it." To Blaze and Twist, he whispered, *"Move. Now."*

Twist and Blaze began shoving and dragging Rachele and Kylie toward the door.

"It's no trouble," Sofia said, tapping her phone's screen. "I just call him."

His guys hauled the girls faster, and Micah brought up the rear.

Sofia spoke into her phone. "Yes, Sofia Maximovna for

Salvatore Grande. No, no. Why you cry? What you mean, Genovese cut him down in the street?"

Micah's mafia war had reached its climax, then. *Excellent.*

Sofia turned to the group of them, still holding the phone to her head. *"Stop. Salvatore Grande is dead. We will make other arrangements for—"*

"Go!" Micah shouted.

He scooped up Kylie in his arms while Blaze threw Rachele over his shoulder in a firefighter's carry, and they sprinted through the warehouse.

Twist took the lead and kicked the exit door, banging it open, and they ran for the SUVs.

Micah threw Kylie in the back seat and jumped into the front.

In his rearview mirror, Twist was turning the SUV's wheels from the driver's seat as Blaze tossed Rachele in the back and dove in after her.

The SUVs sprayed gravel like buckshot as they peeled out. Men with guns emerged from the warehouse, running and shooting but jogging to a stop and leaning over.

Micah floored it, swung the SUV onto the road, and rechecked the rearview mirror.

Sofia Melnik was standing in the parking lot, one hand on her hip, shaking her phone at him.

Kylie leaned over the seat. "You were amazing."

He laughed. *"Thank* you. *Thank* you," like a wiseguy.

She laughed with him.

"And you were *perfect,*" he told her. "The fit about going with us? Extraordinary. *Dead-center perfect.*"

He put his hand up, and Kylie climbed into the front seat and held it as they drove like hell through France toward Monaco.

Kylie was quieter.

The adrenaline flowing through Micah's blood decayed.

He said, "I'm sorry about your mom."

"I am, too," Kylie said. "I didn't know all that. At least I got my sister back."

He checked the rearview mirror one more time. The other black SUV was driving behind them, and Twist raised his hand in a wave.

Micah's phone rang.

Kylie pressed the dot to answer it.

Blaze's panicked voice emerged from the SUV's speakers. "Kylie, tell your sister Micah isn't a hitman! *Ow!* Tell her *he isn't a hitman and we aren't kidnapping her!*"

Kylie yelled into the phone, "Rachele! It's all fine! They're cool. They're friends of mine. Stop hitting him!" To Micah, she said, "Rachele always had a mean punch."

They heard Blaze saying, "I'm going to hold your hands and establish a boundary here. Don't kick! *Don't kick!* It's not okay to hit me. *Ow! Stop it!*"

Kylie yelled to her sister, "It's okay! They're with us! I told Mom they were mafia so she'd *make* us go with them. *Stop hitting him!*"

35

MARCU ARGENTO

MICAH

L ight glared over the computer equipment and walls, and a beam like a spotlight drove into Micah's eyes.

Twist and Micah turned toward the opening door at the back of Twist's darkened computer office on the yacht.

Kylie stuck her head in through the open door. "Micah, you have a phone call."

Kylie and Rachele had been getting reacquainted and spending time together on the main deck. Because Kylie was legally twenty-three as per her shiny new passport, Micah had a lawyer working on getting her legal custody of her sister. They could go home in a few weeks when the paperwork came through.

Blaze had stayed on for a few days of sun and to help with security in case Kylie's mother found them. He was still flinching whenever Rachele made a sudden move, though.

"Is Ostrovsky wanting his painting again?" Micah asked, standing and straightening his trouser legs before he started walking toward her, hand outstretched for the phone.

She bit her lip. "No, but I think you'll want to take this."

Micah emerged into the noontime sun that drenched the city-state of Monaco and the Mediterranean Sea. "Who is it?"

"Vincent Genovese," Kylie said. Her static expression betrayed nothing.

He checked to make sure the phone was muted. "What did he say?"

"I talked to Alessia, who was with Vincent Genovese at the charity thing at the Grimaldi Forum. She's his *daughter*, by the way."

Micah blinked in the sunlight. *"Oh.* His *daughter.* I did not know that."

"Yeah. When they got back to their hotel, all hell broke loose, and not just because some creeper Tommaso Maisto tried to drag her to Italy and force her to marry him because he wanted Vincent Genovese to cut him in on the New York City organized crime action even though he's from Rhode Island—"

"I'm sorry, *what?"* Micah asked.

"Long story. I took care of it. Anyway, there's something else going on, but Alessia doesn't know what. And now her dad wants to talk to you."

Micah smiled as he took the phone. His heart galloped in his chest like a cavalry horse—*go to war, go to war, go to war*—and the sun glistened on the wavelet tips as Micah walked up the deck away from Kylie. "Yes, Mr. Genovese. Good to talk to you again."

The voice on the phone said, "I thought I'd met you before. You've changed in fifteen years, Marcu."

Marcu.

The sea breeze freshened, blowing air cooled from the blue water over the prow of the yacht where Micah stood, facing out to sea. "I'm Micah Shine."

Micah watched a seagull glide over him toward land, turning, and he caught a glimpse of dark curls blowing in the wind.

Kylie was standing on the deck behind him, not close enough that she'd caught his attention, but the wind would have carried his voice to her.

Vincent Genovese asked, "But that is your real name, *Marcu Argento,* isn't it?"

It didn't matter anymore. Vincent Genovese was the guy he'd been hiding from, and if Micah played his cards right, he could *use* this revelation for his own aims.

Yeah, if Kylie was going to make any decisions about him, she should know who she was dealing with. He sure as shit wasn't Micah Shine, the mythological, unconnable honest man with a British accent and no taste for violence.

He put the phone on speaker and moved closer to her, staring right into Kylie's dark eyes. His New York accent rushed back with the bravado and swagger of a kid destined to take over an East Coast organized crime empire. "Yeah, I'm Marcu Argento."

"First, I hear from Salvatore Grande that *my man* Marcu Argento was calling himself Micah Shine and stole priceless paintings from him, and then Sofia Maximovna Melnik is telling people that Marcu Argento, also calling himself Micah Shine, stole her *daughters.*"

"I don't know what you're talking about," he said, mainly for the FBI who'd doubtlessly tapped Genovese's daughter's phone.

"How did you survive, Marcu? You must have been ten years old," he asked.

"Eleven. I was *eleven."*

"Eleven years old, Marcu. Such a tender age."

That asshole. Micah stared straight into Kylie's eyes,

telling her, "When the hitmen you sent walked into my parents' house and started shooting, everyone dove for the ground. They'd been shot. I hadn't. My mother's body fell on top of me. I didn't move, just like they'd taught me. Your goombahs thought I was dead along with my parents, my nonna, Guilia, Francesco, Martina, Silvia, and Davide, so they left."

No images ran through Micah's mind as he spoke.

There were no images. No blood, no torn-apart bodies, no mutilated skulls and chests.

They were gone. Just gone.

Only the words remained.

And the weight.

The terrible, wet, cooling, clammy weight as Micah had struggled to breathe and yet remain absolutely still.

Not a flutter.

Not a twitch.

He said, "Friends of my father came by hours later."

Hours.

He hadn't moved.

On the phone, Genovese scoffed, "Friends of your father? Your father had no friends."

"Yeah, he did. He had lots of friends. They walked right into your organization after you took over. You figured out who they are yet?"

His silence was the answer. Genovese would tear his organization apart from the inside while he was fighting a war.

"They found me, gave me a dead baby's name because that was easier to do that fifteen years ago, and sent me to a boarding school in Europe, where *I* made friends."

"You don't got no friends."

"Oh, I do, Vincent. *You* have no friends. You've got an

organization where some men are afraid of you, and some are waiting for you to show any sign of weakness. You didn't take over the New York area by winning people over. You took it over with betrayal, and that's how you'll go out, too."

He hung up the phone and told Kylie, "Block the number."

She stared at her phone. "But I kind of liked Alessia."

He chuckled. "Don't talk to her father. If you do, he'll threaten you with terrible things that you won't be able to un-hear. Or he'll text you the same. So, I suggest you block the number. If you want to talk to her, do it on a burner phone or over social media with no pictures."

"Yeah, okay." She slid the phone in her pocket and wrapped her arms around his waist. "You okay?"

"Yeah," Micah said, staring out at the sea. "I haven't thought about it in a long time. Getting revenge is more therapeutic than I'd realized."

"Have you gotten revenge?" Kylie asked.

"Not entirely, but I will. I'll tear the whole goddamn world apart if I have to."

36

THE BATTLE OF ANGHIARI BY LEONARDO DA VINCI

KYLIE

TEMPTING
THE
BILLIONAIRE
Romantic Suspense with a Twist

USA TODAY BESTSELLING AUTHOR
BLAIR BABYLON

They decided to order supper in that night.

Kylie and her sister, Rachele, had been living with Micah in his penthouse since they returned from Monaco. Rachele had been enrolled in her new American high school in San Francisco for a few weeks and was somehow getting A's in algebra and C's in French.

In *French.*

Kylie despaired. "You lived *in France* for over three years, and the language of instruction in the schools there was *French.* You are *fluent.* Micah says you don't even have an American accent when you speak it."

Rachele shrugged. "They're teaching it wrong."

She was also making new friends and spending the night at her friend's house that evening.

Micah passed Kylie in the hall and mentioned, "I know we're having supper in, but I've arranged for a nice night. Let's dress up."

Kylie still had the slinky silk dress in her closet from the charity gala in Monaco, so she wore that and did her hair and make-up. The lessons from the cosmetician on Twist's yacht had indeed stuck, and she looked more okay than she used to.

When she came downstairs from their bedroom, Micah was wearing a dark suit with a suspicious lump in one pocket. He kept tapping it, too.

A small table the size of a two-person restaurant table was laid with crystal glasses, white china, and silverware on a snowy tablecloth in the room of his penthouse he called the library.

Bookcases with hundreds of books and other knick-knacks lined the walls.

The Battle of Anghiari by Leonardo da Vinci hung in an enclosed plastic box with its own temperature and humidity controls in a special cut-out area among the bookcases.

The table was just below it.

Kylie took her seat while Micah held her chair for her. "You do like to look at that painting, don't you?"

Micah chuckled. "It's amazing. The fact that it was unknown for this long makes it astonishing."

"Did the analysis on the paint come back?"

"Oh, yes. Chemically, the paint on it matches the paint da Vinci used on other paintings." He glanced at the painting and sighed while smiling. "And I can tell you, that's Leonardo da Vinci's hand."

She laughed at him. "I'm glad."

A waiter came into the library, holding soup plates, and served them.

When he left, Kylie asked him, "When did we get waiters?"

He chuckled. "It's just for tonight. I have a chef in the kitchen making supper, too."

Kylie raised an eyebrow at him as she sipped the soup,

French onion with cheese melting over grilled toast on top. "Well, that's nice. Can we keep him?"

Micah shrugged. "Sure. Why not?"

"I was joking," she told Micah.

"Maybe not Jacques because he's a three-star Michelin chef. I doubt he'd do it. But we can have a private chef in."

Rich-people weirdness shocked Kylie. *"I was kidding."*

A different waiter came in and poured red wine, and they paused the conversation until he left.

"I'm not kidding," Micah said. "It's fine. You're worth it. You're finishing your GED and said you wanted to take college classes. You're busy. I'm busy. Let's have a chef."

"You are traveling a lot." In the month since she'd moved in, he'd been on trips of varying lengths to London, Tokyo, and the Netherlands.

"It'll be easier than figuring out take-away every night."

That was true. "Okay."

"Indeed," Micah said. "Let's get everything settled."

"Oh?" she asked.

Micah rose from his chair and sank to one knee beside the table.

"Oh!"

"Kylie Margaret Miller—" Micah began, his voice rough in his throat.

She said, "I still have not gotten used to that middle name your friend gave me."

"—Ever since we met, I've been dodging bullets and stealing priceless art and daughters, but you have stolen my heart."

"Oh, my God. Tell me you didn't pay someone to write that for you because you got taken."

He cracked up, bowing his head and laughing.

A third waiter came in, holding a pepper mill. She

entered, observed the situation, and U-turned back through the door.

Kylie told him, "Seriously, it's a good thing you're into art and not literature."

Still laughing, Micah asked, "Are you going to let me do this?"

"Do it like a New Yorker. That British accent doesn't sound like you anymore."

Micah shook his arms and cleared his throat. He held her hand and said with a rough, wiseguy New York brogue, "Kylie Margaret Miller, are we doin' this or what?"

Now *that* was her Marcu.

"Yes, Marcu Ragnar Argento, we are doin' this."

He stuck his hand into his suit jacket pocket with the suspicious lump and came out with a ring-sized jewelry box, black velvet. He popped open the top.

The engagement ring inside had an enormous fiery white diamond in the center and smaller diamonds around it in a circle.

"Oh, wow," Kylie said, holding out her hand. "It's beautiful. Where did you get it?"

"I know a guy—"

"Oh, my God, you *know a guy*. Did it fall off the back of a truck, too?"

"I got it in Amsterdam," Micah said as he slid the ring onto her finger. "Good, it fits. An old friend of mine and Arthur took me to the diamond district to buy it. He knows his way around the Netherlands. Caz is a lawyer here in California now. He and his wife, Rox, would love to meet you sometime."

"Yeah, they sound great," Kylie said, dazzled by the diamonds on her finger. She glanced up into Micah's eyes which sparkled just as much as the stones in the ring. "Are you sure? We haven't known each other for very long. It's only been two months."

Micah grinned at her. "When you know, you *know*."

Kylie fretted and finally said what was stomping on her heart. "How do you know I'm not conning you?"

He laughed and stood up, pulling her to stand, too. "If you are, then let it roll. These have been the best two months of my life. And baby, I know I'm not the con artist here so I must be the mark and I'm loving every minute of it. I love you, *cara mia*."

"I love you, too. But, you're okay with my sister and everything?" she asked. "Because now that I've found Rachele, we're kind of a package deal."

He bit his lip with his eyes closed for a minute, then said, "I didn't realize how much I missed having family around. Looking back at the last fifteen years, I don't know how I stood it. She's my little sister now, too."

Micah bent and kissed her, his lips soft on hers, then deepened the kiss.

When he broke it off, Kylie was gasping and kind of wanted to clear the table, but there were also waiters right outside the door.

Instead, she blurted, "I'm not conning you."

Micah smiled down at her, touching the edges of her face. "I know."

37

THE ANNUNCIATION BY LORENZO DI CREDI

MICAH

Micah strode into the ice-white office in downtown Manhattan, watching Mary Varvara Bell as he approached her desk.

She stood and offered him her hand to shake as he neared. "Marcu Argento."

He shook her hand firmly but not like an asshole trying to crush it, and she returned the handshake with the same confident pressure. "Dr. Bell, a pleasure to see you again."

"You outdid yourself with this assignment. Salvatore Grande is dead, along with most of his capos, and Vincent Genovese's operation is in chaos. More than half of his members are dead, and he appears to have decided that half of his remaining members are a problem and about to have a headache. In addition, the *Chekhovskaya* bratva is in disarray because there was a power vacuum on one side when Sofia Melnik appeared weak. She's been toppled, and the other members are infighting for power. We have made excellent inroads into all territories. It's truly an outstanding accomplishment."

"*Thank* you," Micah said and looked off to the side. "*Thank* you."

"And I thank you for the bonus prize, this lovely work of art." Dr. Bell gestured toward the painting of *The Annunciation* by Lorenzo di Credi that hung on her wall in an alcove where direct sunlight wouldn't hit it.

Again, the Old Master painting was properly preserved in a climate-controlled plastic chamber with a small digital display to confirm the temperature and humidity inside because Mary Varvara Bell was not a monster.

She continued, "I can confidently say it's a unique gift that I'll treasure."

"I'm glad you like it." Micah sat in the chair in front of her desk. "You said the books would be open?"

"Indeed. I am pleased to have you as a valuable member of White Holdings, Inc. We don't have you burn a picture of St. Paul and recite vows of omertà. I hope you're not too disappointed."

He laughed. "I always found the theater of it a bit much."

She smiled. "Our business, like most grown-up business, is on a handshake."

Micah stood and reached for another handshake, a firmer one that meant much more.

With that, Micah was inducted into the next criminal syndicate he intended to burn to the ground.

Mary Varvara Bell gestured behind herself, and a door opened. "You might as well begin meeting other members of our organization with whom you'll be working. I believe you already know my nephew."

Logan Bell walked into the office, a shock of darkness in the snowy whiteness of the office with his black hair and black suit. "Hello, Micah."

Micah wasn't goddamn shocked at all. "Hello, Logan."

38

LETTER

BLAZE ROBINSON

B laze Robinson was sitting in one of the living rooms in what other people would call a mansion in the Lincoln Park neighborhood of Chicago, reading a newspaper on a tablet, when a butler delivered an envelope to him. "It came by courier, sir."

"Thank you," Blaze said, setting aside the tablet and looking at the envelope.

The creamy stationery was thick in his hands like a wedding invitation, perhaps, but it was a letter-sized envelope, not square.

He opened it.

Read it.

And called his goddamned lawyer.

WHAT COMES NEXT?
Blaze (Twisted Billionaires #5)

Blaze Robinson is the third man in the Twisted Billionaires series. Will he be sucked into the organized crime bratva, too?

Get the exciting next book in the Twisted Billionaires series!

Want to start at the beginning?
Start with *Working Stiff*.
For the full reading experience,
get the Working Stiff **Audiobook narrated by Joe Arden.**

The Billionaires in Disguise Universe (BIDU) by Blair Babylon: Fall in love with mysterious, dirty-sexy billionaires in exotic locales in this interconnected romance novel series that will leave you breathless on the edge of your seat from the nail-biting suspense, shocking plot twists, *and more.*

When Rox was hired, she told her smoking-hot boss Cash that she was married, *but she's not.* Now, three years later, she's kind of accidentally living with him, and he's being a perfect gentleman, *dang it.*

Everybody in the office said that Cash was a heartbreaker, that he'd bump her and dump her, so Rox decided not to become a statistic. She went out and bought herself some rings of the finest cubic zirconia so that she could work with Cash, who was several inches over six feet tall, emerald-eyed, ripped, gorgeous, his tailored suit clinging to his athletic body, sporting a British accent, and *loaded.*

It had seemed like such a good idea at the time.

But now, three years later, she and Cash have become friends. They travel together for work often, and they're the best of buddies.

When Rox gets thrown out of her apartment, Cash insists that she come live with him until they can find her a place because that's what friends do.

Now, even though everyone insists that Cash never goes after married women, something about him has changed. There are little touches, little slips, and Rox is more and more tempted to tell hunky, gorgeous Cash that she never was married.

And then he'll take her and break her, and then he'll walk away, and then she'll lose her job, and she still hasn't found a place to live.

And yet, every time he looks at her with mischief in his dark green eyes, every time they're teasing and it somehow turns into tickling, every time she swats at him and somehow ends up in his arms, she wants so much to risk everything.

What's a working stiff to do when she falls in love with her friend, the boss?

INCLUDES YOUR FAVORITE TROPES:

✓ Friends to Lovers

✓ Secret Royals

✓ Over the Top Romantic Suspense

✓ and always, Thrillers that Bang!

USA Today Bestselling Author Blair Babylon writes bestselling romance books that will free your mind. These five star billionaire boss, enemies to lovers, friends to lovers, and romantic comedy romantic novels quickly turn into suspense thriller books that will make your pulse pound and soothe your heart. Whether the couple are trapped in a pretend marriage or there's only one bed, Blair's books are like romancing your own duke, mister, or billionaire. Some are an ugly cry, some are an affair to remember with a king or a prince, and some are a few shades darker, but all are unputdownable. Fans of Danielle Steel, E.L. James, Helen Hardt, Anna Todd, and Charlotte Byrd will love Blair's romantic books and romance audiobooks. Set your heart free and download these fantastic, complete series!

Get *Working Stiff* from your favorite bookstore!
For the full reading experience,
get the Working Stiff **Audiobook**
narrated by Joe Arden.

~

Get notices of new releases,
special discounts, freebies, and
deleted scenes and epilogues
from Blair Babylon!
Go to:
https://blairbabylon.com/emailbx
On your favorite browser.

A NOTE FROM BLAIR

Hello there!

Thank you so much for reading the story of Micah Shine and Kylie Miller, the second duet of the *Twisted Billionaires* series. I hope you loved Micah Shine.

If you haven't read Twist's story, you should! Start with *Twisted Billionaire!*

Special shout out and THANK YOU to Priyanka Mehtani who won a charity auction for her name to be given to the character. Her generosity has helped many people, and she's wonderful.

If you're new to my books, the *Twisted Billionaire* series is part of the overall *Billionaires in Disguise Universe (BID)*.

Each individual mini-series stands by itself, so look for the "Book #1" in each series. Some are collected in boxed sets, so keep an eye out for those collections. I've written over 40 books in the greater BID universe and have no intention of stopping anytime soon, so you have lots of books to fall in love with!

Here's a list of the first books in each mini-series.

Working Stiff ~ Working Stiff Audiobook - *Casimir van Amsberg, attorney to the stars with a little royal secret.*

Stiff Drink ~ Stiff Drink Audiobook - *Arthur Finch-Hatten, Casimir's English buddy who is not just an idle, rich nobleman.*

Every Breath You Take - Rock Star Xan Valentine is hiding more than you'd think.

Once Upon A Time ~ Once Upon A Time Audiobook - Flicka von Hannover's story. Bodyguard romance

Billionaires in Disguise (Wulf and Rae) - The first BID book I wrote, kind of the lynchpin in the middle.

Falling Hard Do you like your romance a little . . . darker? This one is painted in the darkest shades of grey.

What A Girl Wants - The first of the Rock Stars in Disguise (RSID) series, but there's a point where the RSID plotline intersects with the BID plotline. You'll see.

Twisted Billionaires - A mysterious organized crime boss blackmails four budding billionaires into joining her organization, but they plan to destroy her evil empire.

Dragons & Magic - Do you link your romance heroes <u>hot?</u> *Like, really HOT? Like, really-really-okay these guys can actually breathe fire. PNR.*

The chronological reading list is here at my website, https://blairbabylon.com/reading-order/ . Really, each of the mini-series can be read by themselves, so you don't have to worry about doing it perfectly. But if you want the best, total experience, check out that reading order and start with *Working Stiff ~ Working Stiff* Audiobook .

If you want to know when I publish a new book or have a sale, sign up for my newsletter at https://blairbabylon. com/emailbx .

I also have a Facebook reader group, Blair's Babes' VIP Room, where we have fun and talk about books. I hang around in there and answer questions. A couple of times per year, we have an "ABA," or Ask Blair Anything, but I reserve the right to waffle if there are spoilers involved. I also do giveaways. My reader group gets the best prize boxes. We talk about a lot of books in there, and other authors drop in for their giveaways. It's a fun and positive place.

Make sure you're signed up for my **NEWSLETTER** (https://blairbabylon.com/emailbx) so you'll know when I have a new book out! Mailing list subscribers get FREE access to special epilogues and books that there's no other way to get.

Thank you again for reading.

Love,

Blair Babylon

ABOUT BLAIR BABYLON

What order should I read Blair's Books in?
https://blairbabylon.com/reading-order/
for ALL of Blair Babylon's Books.

Blair's Website: Lots of Fun News, Extras, Reading Order,
List of Blair's Books, and More!
www.BlairBabylon.com

About Blair Babylon

Blair Babylon is an award-winning author who used to publish literary fiction. Because reviews of her mainstream fiction usually included the caveat that there was too much deviant sex in her novels, she decided to abandon all literary pretensions, let her freak flag fly, and write hot, sexy romance novels. She's having much more fun now.